Agent Rhone Craigson has known about shifters for nearly a decade. He also knows there's a group of them currently hiding out in the remote bayous of Louisiana. When several missing persons reports come to Rhone's attention, all from that area, his curiosity is piqued . . . along with a healthy dose of concern. For the safety of, well, everyone, shifters need to stay under the radar.

Rhone needs to know if the shifter group is involved in the disappearance of humans in that area. Due to the fact that there's a mole in the CIA, feeding the military sensitive information, he decides to visit the shifters in person. When Rhone arrives, he finds the group surprisingly welcoming and forthcoming. Joining them for a meal, he spots a cute, dirty-blond-haired twink that causes an unexpected dose of attraction, who's introduced as Mickey, a meerkat shifter.

When Mickey claims they're mates, Rhone knows that means Mickey expects them to bond and live as a couple. While Rhone can admit that he wouldn't mind getting to know the little shifter, so much is going on within the agency. Can he discover the mole to ensure Mickey's safety, or is walking away the safer option?

A Meerkat for the Agent
Copyright © 2023 Charlie Richards
ISBN: 978-1-4874-3886-9
Cover art by Angela Waters

Published by eXtasy Books Inc

Look for us online at:
www.eXtasybooks.com

A Meerkat for the Agent Kontra's Menagerie: Book Thirty-Five

By

Charlie Richards

CHAPTER ONE

"Another one?"

"Afraid so, sir."

Agent Rhone Craigson sighed deeply, rubbing the bridge of his nose. Lowering his hand, he flipped open the file's cover. He frowned as he took in the picture of a rough-looking, middle-aged man with cruel eyes.

"He looks like he'd be the one to make people go missing, not the other way around," Rhone commented absently. Upon hearing Agent Carlton Reed's snort of amusement, Rhone grimaced. "Sorry. That was stereotyping."

Carlton chuckled as he shrugged. "You're not wrong. The guy looks like an asshole." The technical analyst crossed his arms over his chest as he cocked his head. "Why is this area so important to you? Is it related to a case I haven't heard about?"

Rhone shook his head. "Not really." The hairs on the back of his neck stood on end as unease churned in his gut. Smirking at Carlton, Rhone forced his tone to come out even. "And if you hadn't heard about the case, I wouldn't be able to tell you about it anyway."

"So this is a personal matter?" The slender dark-haired man grinned. "That's not standard procedure, ya know."

Yup. I'm definitely starting to not trust this guy. Too bad, because he's good at his job.

Narrowing his eyes, Rhone pinned Carlton with a hard look. "The area came up on the radar of the FBI, and I recognized it because I have a friend in the area," he lied smoothly.

"I just wanted to know if there was an issue down there." Tapping the picture of the nasty-looking man in the folder, he added, "And according to your find, several people have disappeared around there."

Good thing I didn't have Carlton look into the issue of the science lab burning to the ground.

Due to the fact that Rhone knew there was a mole in the CIA—a mole feeding information to a questionable section of the military—Rhone didn't use the same technical analyst on more than one case at a time. That way, if information made its way back to the military, he would know who to go after. It was probably too simple of a plan, but it was the best he and his boss, Deputy Director Lawrence Reiste, had at the moment. Between them and Agent Slade Wellington, the man Rhone often ended up paired with, they hoped to close in on the mole.

"Well, I'll keep an eye on it for you," Carlton told him, his hands lifted in placation. "And let you know if anyone else pops up as missing around there." Frowning, Carlton cocked his head. "Should we notify the FBI that there's something hinky going on there? I mean, these sorts of guys don't seem to be the standard for a kidnapper, but maybe he likes to torture tough guys before disposing of them in the swamp or something."

Rhone closed the file and relaxed back in his chair. "I'll handle it," he said with a nod. "Thanks, Agent Reed. If I need anything further on the three you've already given me, I'll contact you."

"Sure." Carlton must have recognized a dismissal when he heard it, for he turned away and started toward the door. "Good luck, sir." Pausing at the door, he looked over his shoulder at Rhone, a wry smile curving his lips. "I don't envy you having to work with another department."

Scoffing, Rhone simply dipped his chin in a nod. Relief filled him when Carlton closed the door behind him, leaving him alone. He knew the technical analyst thought he would pass the information on to the FBI, but that wasn't his plan at all.

Rhone opened a drawer and pulled out two other files. Placing them on top of the third, he picked them all up. He rose to his feet and headed out of his office, locking the door behind him.

A few minutes later, Rhone stood before Deputy Director Reiste's office door. He knocked. When he heard his boss order him to enter, he did so.

Closing and locking the door behind him, Rhone watched Lawrence hang up his phone. The deputy director lifted his finger to his lips, and Rhone waited patiently. The deputy director pulled an electronic device from his desk drawer, set it on his desk, and pushed a button.

While Rhone couldn't hear anything, he knew what the device was doing. In the off chance that someone had placed a listening device in Lawrence's office, all it would pick up would be white noise. Rhone knew he would be able to speak freely of a sensitive subject that so few humans knew about.

Paranormals.

"What do you have?" Lawrence asked, glancing toward the files while indicating the seat before his desk.

Rhone moved toward him. As he placed the files on his boss's desk, he settled in the chair. Relaxing back, he crossed his legs before him.

"A third man disappeared in the Louisiana bayou," Rhone stated, tapping his forefinger against the arm of the chair.

As Lawrence pulled the files toward him, he commented, "People disappear in the swamp all the time." Opening the top one, he arched a brow. "A young man. Twenty years old. Josiah LaFleur." Lawrence met his gaze. "This man disappeared a few years ago."

"I had him checked into because someone in Kontra's gang is looking for him," Rhone explained. Pointing at the files, he added, "The other two men disappeared near the area they're staying. One was a security guard for a private company hired by a facility that burned to the ground a few months back. The last man lived in a small town near where they're staying."

"You think Kontra's people are involved?" Lawrence asked softly, pushing the file aside to open the next one. He glanced up at him. "Chase Ingerson. Ex-military."

"I'm not sure," Rhone admitted, shaking his head slowly. "I'd like to go down there and check." Holding Lawrence's gaze, he added, "He did invite me to visit, after all."

"Don't you have his number?"

Dipping his chin, Rhone admitted, "I do." He fought back the feel of the heat threatening to rise up his neck. "But with our mole problem, I don't trust the phone lines."

"I understand." Nodding slowly, Lawrence returned his attention to the final file. His brows shot up. "Herbert Broussard. He looks older than his twenty-eight years. Sure on the age?" Lawrence refocused on him.

"According to Agent Reed's information." Pointing at the file, he told him, "That just happened a couple of days ago." He grimaced. "I know it's stereotyping, but I kinda wonder if he was a bigoted asshole that got on the wrong side of Kontra's gang."

Rhone knew that Kontra Belikov was a grizzly shifter—a being who shared his psyche with a big bear that he could turn into at will. He led a group of gay or bisexual men. On the surface, they appeared to be a biker gang, which helped keep questioners away.

"As amusing as I'd find that," Deputy Director Reiste began, a smirk curving his lips. "Assholes are entitled to their opinions. Damn pesky freedom of speech and all." He closed the files and stacked them. "You have my permission to head down there." As Lawrence slid the files back toward him, he added, "Under the radar, though. Don't go as an agent. Find out what's up."

"I'd love a vacation," Rhone stated, managing to keep most of the sarcasm out of his voice. He knew he was a workaholic, but if he was taking vacation days, he wanted it to actually be a vacation.

Lawrence pinned a narrow-eyed gaze at him, but amusement danced within the depths of his brown eyes. "I'll find a way to make it up to you."

Rhone nodded. "Thanks."

He rose to his feet, knowing Lawrence would follow through, too. The wiry black man had been the deputy director for his department for a little over a year, and he was worlds better than his prior one. He'd always found him to be a man of his word.

"Are you leaving today?"

Picking up the files, Rhone nodded. "I'll finish out my day to alleviate suspicion," he told him. "Then fly out this evening, rent a car, and drive to the place where I think Kontra is hiding out."

"Where is that?"

"Uh . . ." Frowning, Rhone flipped open the report on Chase. "Chase's last known location was near the home of Olson Caynar, a man who'd also worked at the facility that went up. Although he'd quit a week prior." Rhone shrugged. "From travel records, Chase was on vacation when the facility went, so he might have gone to Olson to see if he knew what had happened."

"Hmmm . . . What *did* happen there?"

Rhone winced, pausing where he stood before his boss's desk. "According to my last contact with Kontra, there were shifters in that facility. Shifters being experimented on—"

"By those assholes being funded by that shadow branch of the military?" Lawrence cut in. "The one the mole works for?"

Jerking a nod, Rhone confirmed, "The same. Also, the same one General Sackett was involved with."

"Don't those assholes know how difficult their stupidity is making containing the secret of shifters and other paranormals?" Lawrence grumbled, running a hand over his face.

"If they get super soldiers out of it, I don't suppose they care." Rhone felt his anger surge, and it took every bit of his self-control to keep it contained and off his face. "They want to take advantage of their gifts to help themselves . . . and make a shitload of money."

Lawrence arched one black brow.

"My apologies, sir," Rhone quickly stated. He rarely gave in to the urge to curse, especially while at work.

"Your words are true." Lawrence held up a hand, palm out, while pressing the button to turn off the dampener. "Your request for vacation has been approved," Lawrence stated. "Enjoy your time off."

"Thank you, Director Reiste. I appreciate it."

Then Rhone headed out of the office, closing the door behind him. He returned to his own office and finished out his day.

Stepping off the plane in Baton Rouge, Louisiana, Rhone headed toward the luggage claim. He hefted his carry-on bag over one shoulder. Rhone didn't need to pick up a bag, but according to the map, that was where the rental pick-ups were.

Rhone stepped up to the counter, pleased there wasn't a line. After getting the keys to the truck he'd reserved, he headed outside. The hot, muggy air wrapped around him, and he quickly shucked his jacket and draped it over his arm.

Finding his vehicle, Rhone climbed in. He placed his jacket and bag on the floor of the passenger side. After firing it up, he headed away from the airport.

At the first opportunity, Rhone stopped at a convenience store. He purchased a bag of peanuts, a bag of sunflower seeds, and a six-pack of water. Back in the rented truck, Rhone pulled up a map on the vehicle's GPS system.

Finding where he wanted to go, Rhone headed on his way, looking forward to not only the several-hour drive, but finally meeting Kontra Belikov.

Taking the last bend in the road, Rhone swept his gaze over Olson's large Victorian home hidden deep in the bayou. His gut clenched as he took in the dozens of men milling around the area, and he wondered if he'd made a huge mistake by not calling ahead. As Rhone parked, his fingers itched to grab his *Glock* from his bag, which his federal credentials had allowed him to take on board the plane.

There were several men throwing a football back and forth. A number were in the garage, tinkering on a couple of the over a dozen motorcycles within it. Several were standing beside the house, seeming to be studying the old siding. More were even further away, milling around a fire where they appeared to be roasting something on the spit situated over the open flame.

A trio approached his vehicle, and Rhone took in the middle figure—a large imposing-looking man with thick dark hair peppered with what appeared to be silver-gray flecks. He sported a thick goatee around firm lips and peered at him with intense dark eyes.

From Alpha Declan's description—a wolf shifter Rhone had worked with on several occasions—that was Alpha Kontra.

Makes sense.

Girding up his courage, Rhone eased from his rented truck, closing the door behind him. "Alpha Kontra?" He decided to go with the direct approach. Holding out his hand, he stated, "I'm Agent Craigson. Please, call me Rhone."

Instantly, Kontra's hard features eased. A wide smile curved his lips. "Agent Craigson. Rhone." Kontra took his hand in a relaxed grip. "It's fantastic to finally meet you." Releasing him, he used that hand to indicate the scarred dark-haired man to his right and the intimidating black man to his left. "This is my beta, Sam, and my head enforcer, Mutegi."

"Gentlemen," Rhone greeted with a dip of his chin to each man.

Kontra rested his hands on his hips and smirked. "I can't imagine a CIA agent would come all this way just to say hi." With a wave toward the house, he offered, "Come in. We'll get drinks, and you can tell me what brings you way out here."

Feeling his tension ease at Kontra's friendly demeanor, Rhone agreed and followed him toward the house.

CHAPTER TWO

M ickey fumbled the football in his hands a little before catching it securely. Having never thrown a ball in his life, he was still struggling with the activity. The guys who were teaching him were patient and kind about it, though. They showed him the proper way to hold the oblong object as well as the way to rotate his arm for a good loft.

Adjusting his fingers on the laces, Mickey readied himself. He cocked his arm back and threw. The ball flew through the air toward Adam—a white tiger shifter—with quite a bit of wobble in the spiral. The big, blond shifter still had no trouble catching the ball.

"Nicely done," Adam praised, grinning at him. "You're gettin' it." He quickly zinged the ball to Ronnie—a moose shifter—as he added, "You'll be a pro in no time."

Ronnie caught the ball. The big brown-haired man looked intimidating until he winced. Scowling at Adam, he shook out one of his hands. "Dial it back, Adam," he grumbled, shaking his head. "You nearly took my hand off."

Adam just laughed.

With a roll of his eyes, Ronnie turned and threw the ball toward his mate, Hector—an armadillo shifter. His toss was obviously much lighter as it soared gracefully through the air in a slow arc. Hector easily caught it, then turned and passed the ball to Adam's mate, Noah. Noah was also a moose shifter and Ronnie's older brother, even though Ronnie was the larger of the two by a couple of inches. While extremely young by shifter standards at only twenty-three years old,

Ronnie was already exhibiting dominant tendencies, but their leader, Kontra Belikov, easily kept the burgeoning alpha in line.

Finally, Noah threw the ball back to Mickey. The sound of an approaching engine—an unfamiliar engine—caught Mickey's attention, distracting him. He completely flubbed the catch. The ball bounced off the fingers of his left hand, hit the ground at an odd angle, and rolled away from him.

"Oops."

Mickey felt his cheeks heat as he went after the ball. While picking it up, he noticed all the shifters in animal form fled into the woods. A few of them still didn't have the ability to shift. Some would change to human form, grab clothes they'd had stashed in the area, and return dressed.

Having been one of half a dozen shifters rescued from an illegal research facility run by shady scientists, Mickey actually felt grateful. He figured he was one of the lucky ones. While it had hurt to be experimented on by the assholes, he'd only been there a few weeks. Once their drugs had worn off, Mickey had been able to shift normally.

Others weren't so lucky. They'd been held by witches for many years. Between spells, herbs, and beatings, they were struggling to regain their human forms.

Mickey knew that was why Kontra was still in the area. Normally, his group were a semi-nomadic biker gang. They traveled the country, helping when they could while taking out assholes along the way. Kontra was waiting for those stuck in animal form to be able to shift freely.

During that time, they were staying at the home of Olson Caynar and helping him fix up his aging Victorian home. The place was really beginning to take shape, both inside and out.

"You okay, Mickey?" Adam asked, taking a few steps toward him.

The move and question yanked Mickey out of his thoughts.

"Yeah." He pulled his attention away from the parking truck, doing his best to ignore the unease in his gut. He knew Alpha Kontra would take care of it. "Just got stuck in my head."

Mickey threw the ball to Adam, his spiral a bit better that time. As the ball was passed around again, he saw his alpha smile and greet the blond man who exited the truck. His unease settled, seeing that Kontra appeared to know him and was acting welcoming.

In Mickey's mind, strangers were normally a bad thing . . . but he had his reasons for that.

Catching the ball, Mickey continued to keep a bit of his attention on the blond accompanying Alpha Kontra into the house. He couldn't seem to help how his gut churned just a smidge for a new reason. The blond was big and handsome, with broad shoulders and nicely muscled legs encased in faded jeans. His short-sleeved shirt showed off well-developed biceps and a trim waist.

Then, just as the man slipped through the door in front of Enforcer Mutegi, his scent wafted across the clearing and teased Mickey's nose. The ball he'd been in the process of throwing to Adam went wide right. Mickey couldn't find it in himself to care as Adam had to run and jump to catch the ball.

It really was an impressive effort by the tiger shifter.

Instead, Mickey remained riveted on the closed front door. His heart pounded wildly in his chest. His dick, which had remained dormant from the second he'd been found kissing a human boy by an enforcer in his mob, stirred swiftly to life.

"Mickey?"

He didn't respond to Noah's concerned-sounding call. He couldn't. His mouth had gone dry, his body still reacting to the delicious aroma of their guest.

Oh gods. How is this possible?

Mickey had watched others in Kontra's gang find their mates — the other halves of their souls. A shifter's mate was a person designed by Fate herself, the person capable of bonding with him or her. That would twine their life-threads, and they would forge a life together as a couple.

"Mickey?" Adam's hand coming down on his shoulder yanked his attention to the much larger shifter. Peering at him with worry in his blue eyes, Adam asked, "Is everything okay? Do you know that man?"

Ronnie growled, cracking his knuckles. "Is he from your old mob?" His dark brows furrowed as he glared toward the house. "Is he one of the guys who ran you out?"

"Settle down, handsome," Hector murmured, resting his hand on Ronnie's forearm. "Let the man explain."

Noah rested his hand on Mickey's back, rubbing gently. "Take a deep breath and relax," he encouraged. "Whatever it is, we'll help."

All four men were crowded around him. When they'd moved, Mickey had no idea. Noah's touch relaxed him, the tension draining from him.

"I-I think . . ." Mickey began, then stalled. He could hardly imagine it, yet voice it.

"You think?" Adam pressed. "Think what, Mickey?"

Mickey swallowed hard, wrapping his arms around his waist. "I-I think, um, think that man" — he paused to peer at the house before finishing on a whisper — "that man might be my mate."

"Your mate?" Ronnie repeated, sounding an odd mixture of incredulity and surprise.

Adam grinned widely and whooped. "Your mate?" He sounded jovial. "That's fantastic!" Peering toward the house, Adam stated firmly, "Well, then you need to meet him." He took a step toward the house. "Come on."

Noah grabbed Adam's arm. "Whoa, big guy. It looks like he's in a meeting with Kontra." He furrowed his brows, looking worried. "And we don't even know who he is."

Scoffing, Adam wrapped his arm around Noah's shoulders. "Doesn't matter who he is, my love." He gave his lover a hungry smile. "If that's Mickey's mate, then he's perfect for him." His voice lowered further. "Just like you're perfect for me."

Then Adam sealed his mouth over Noah's. Wrapping his other arm around his lover's waist and reeling him in tight. Their kiss went from gentle to nuclear in half a second.

Mickey looked away, spotting the grimace on Ronnie's face.

"You'd think after so many years, I'd be used to that," Ronnie muttered. After a side-eyed glance their way, he turned his attention to the house. "But I'm not. That's my brother."

Hector slid his arm around Mickey's waist even as he threaded his fingers into Ronnie's. "Come on, guys. Let's see if anyone inside has some info on our guest." As he spoke, he began urging Mickey toward the front porch, Ronnie easily joining his mate.

Mickey felt stiff, his legs threatening to buckle. A tremble worked through him. Unease, excitement, and arousal churned within him, and he suddenly felt the need to puke.

"A-Aren't I too young?" Mickey whispered, shaking his head in disbelief. "I-I'm only twenty-seven."

"And I'm twenty-three," Ronnie pointed out with a shrug. "It's rare that a young shifter finds his mate, but it does happen."

Mickey nodded absently, his mind still reeling.

When Mickey had heard the elders of his mob talk about finding their fated mate, it had been in wishful tones. They acted as if a shifter needed to wait hundreds of years for it to happen. It had been so long since someone in Mickey's old mob had found a fated mate that some of the younger generation didn't even believe in them anymore, considering them old wives' tales.

Mickey had thought that, too. Although he'd never admitted it to his new friends. Instead, when he'd been rescued by Kontra's gang, he'd been shocked to discover it *was* true. Many members had met their fated mate . . . and they were even gay and bisexual.

Never would his mob have believed that gay shifters would have a fated mate. Hell, that was the whole reason he'd been run off. They believed he and his ilk were abominations.

And now . . . I may have scented my fated mate. Oh my gods.

Unable to help himself, Mickey wrenched from Hector's grasp. He sprinted to the side of the house and bent over a bush. Seconds later, his stomach rebelled, and he expelled the contents of his breakfast.

Mickey registered the gentle hand on his back, rubbing in soothing circles. Mortified, he didn't bother trying to open his eyes. Instead, he rested his forearm against the aging siding and pressed his sweaty forehead against it.

The feel of the cold cloth against the back of his neck felt amazing. His skin goose bumped, but he didn't mind. Even the chill that went down his spine as the wet cloth trickled droplets of water under his shirt was welcome.

Slowly, Mickey felt the bile ease from his throat, returning to his stomach, where it should be.

Mickey took in a deep, shuddering breath.

"Hey, Mickey."

Mickey registered Eli's voice. The Burmese python shifter was the pack doctor. He was mated to a small wolf shifter, who was also named Sam.

"How about some water to rinse out your mouth," Eli offered softly, pressing a chilly bottle against the back of the fingers on the hand he had wrapped around his waist. "It'll make you feel better."

"I-I'm so y-young," Mickey whispered, glancing around the group, seeing a mixture of worried and understanding looks. "I'm a virgin," he squeaked out. "What if h-he doesn't want me?"

Sam continued to rub his back as Eli massaged the back of his neck through the cloth. "Of course your mate will want you," Sam murmured, giving him an encouraging smile. "And since Fate chose him, then he'll be happy to teach you everything you need to know."

Another idea hit Mickey, causing his gut to churn anew. "Wh-What if I was wrong?"

Mickey's meerkat chittered in his mind, sounding annoyed, telling him in no uncertain terms that they were not wrong. The human inside was their mate.

"Do you really think you're wrong?" Eli asked softly, his dark eyes holding his gaze steadily.

Micky sighed even as he took the water Eli offered him. "No. I-I think he's my mate."

"Then let's get you cleaned up," Sam urged. "While Adam finds out more about your mate."

With Sam and Eli bracketing him, Mickey allowed them to guide him into the house. He didn't look around. He didn't want to meet the gazes of any of the others. Mickey bet he was the only shifter in history to throw up upon scenting their mate.

Gods, how embarrassing.

CHAPTER THREE

"So that facility was run by a group of scientists affiliated with the military," Rhone snarled, shaking his head. His hand clenched on the tumbler of tequila he held in his hand. "How the fuck do they keep setting this shit up without us tracking them?"

"Too many rich assholes funding them," Sam grumbled, rubbing his thumb along the scar etched into his cheek. The large beta of the shifter gang glared at his drink as he brought it to his lips. Before taking a drink, he mumbled, "Damn entitled fuckers."

Rhone could only guess at his reasons for seeming to take it so personally. Keeping his mouth shut, he took a sip of his own drink. As he swallowed, a soft knock sounded from the other side of the closed door to the study-turned-office.

Mutegi rose and headed toward the door.

"There always seems to be some group out there who wants to persecute or use another group for their own ends," Kontra commented, barely giving Mutegi a glance as he opened the door and slipped out of the room. "The fact that the group being persecuted are more powerful than humans"—Kontra lifted a hand in placation—"no offense"—before lowering it again—"even if we are in the minority, will cause global repercussions if news of us ever gets out." With a soft growl, he admitted, "Most paranormals have absolutely no desire to have our presence revealed to humans at large."

"For which we appreciate," Rhone replied, nodding. "The

few at the CIA who know are completely on board with keeping your secret." Rubbing his hand over his thigh, he shook his head. "God, I can only imagine the wars, the bloodshed, if the existence of paranormals ever got out."

"Witch hunts everywhere," Sam stated bluntly with a scoff. "Everyone and their brother would suddenly become certain their next-door neighbor was a shifter or vampire."

With a snort, Rhone nodded. "So after you took out that facility, you ended up stopping Chase from hurting Olson because he was the mate of one of your people."

Rhone saw Kontra nod, and Rhone moved on. After all, he knew how important a paranormal viewed their mate—the other half of their soul. The paranormal considered that person the most important person in their world.

"And Herbert tried to kill his brother, Horace, who is also mated to one of your people?"

"Right. We—"

"Alpha Kontra, I apologize for interrupting," Mutegi cut in. He crooked a finger at the shifter alpha. "A moment, please?"

Rhone noticed Kontra's brow twitch just a little, betraying his surprise. Still, the large male rose from his seat. He crossed to Mutegi and dipped his head the couple of inches, allowing the head enforcer to whisper into his ear.

"Hmmm, really?" Kontra sounded surprised.

"Yes, Alpha."

Kontra grunted and patted Mutegi on the shoulder. "Interesting." He straightened and turned to peer at Rhone. "Do you have a room booked locally?"

Surprised at the question, Rhone shook his head. "I thought about it. I thought about camping, too." He rarely had the opportunity to enjoy nature, and he wanted to take advantage of the forced vacation. With a wry smile, Rhone admitted, "I'd hoped, considering your nomadic lifestyle, that you'd have some camping gear I could borrow."

"Sure do," Kontra replied, nodding. "This place only has so many bedrooms, so there are plenty of tents set up out back that you probably didn't even notice." Turning back to Mutegi, Kontra asked, "How's the food coming? My stomach's telling me it's about time to eat. Is Tim done training with Draven and Evan?"

Mutegi smiled. "I will find out."

"Thanks." Kontra patted his enforcer's back as the man opened the door, leaving it open that time. "Want Sam to refresh your drink, Rhone?" Kontra asked, holding up his own nearly empty tumbler. "Then we can head out back and see what's grilling." The alpha patted his flat belly. "I think I'm about ready for a steak."

As if on cue, Sam rose and headed toward the sideboard.

"Uh, sure." Rhone downed the rest of his drink, enjoying the taste of the high-end tequila. "But you don't really have to put me up." Never would Rhone have imagined the alpha shifter would offer to let him stay with his pack. "I don't want to be an inconvenience."

Kontra waved his hand as if shooing away his objections. "Putting up an ally against those trying to harm our kind is never an inconvenience," he told him, heading toward him. "It'll also give us the opportunity to share with you what else is going on in the paranormal world. You'll need to prepare your people."

"Prepare them for what?" Rhone couldn't help but ask, not resisting when Kontra plucked his tumbler from his hand. Concern filled him. "Have more shady military branches popped up?"

That would completely suck. Learning about one had been a rough enough blow for him and his superiors. Then they'd discovered that one of their own—an agent named Haroldson—had been using his access to capture and sell shifters.

Fortunately, while taking him out, they'd been able to remove a number of others in shifter trafficking, too.

Too bad more always seem to keep cropping up.

Unfortunately, Rhone knew that was the way of greed and power — those who had it always seemed to want more, and those who thought they deserved it would do anything to get it.

"Afraid so," Kontra told him, placing the tumbler on the sideboard. "Have you heard of General Saxx?"

Rhone shook his head. "Can't say that I have." He watched Sam refill all three of their tumblers. "How's he involved?"

"Sadly, he's connected with an ex-councilman who went rogue." Kontra handed him back his drink. "We caught him and put him down. Our spy gave us a few names our ex-councilman was in contact with." Wincing, Kontra admitted, "General Saxx is working with another scientist. We're in the process of taking out their facilities, but we don't know if we're getting to them all."

"More always seem to pop up," Sam grumbled once more.

Kontra gripped Sam's shoulder and squeezed. "That's life, my friend."

Sam nodded. "Sadly, yes."

Indicating the door, Kontra stated, "Come on. We'll share what we know over a meal."

"Okay." Rhone followed Sam out of the room, all the while wondering how to keep any information he learned secure. "I appreciate your willingness to collaborate."

To Rhone's surprise, Kontra chuckled. "I'm sure collaborating will be vital in the future."

Rhone glanced over his shoulder at Kontra as he turned left, following Sam. The bigger male wore a serious expression, but there was something in his eyes that Rhone couldn't read. He wondered what was going on in the big shifter's brain.

Considering shifters could live for centuries, Rhone wondered what he'd seen over the years.

Maybe I'll get up the nerve to ask.

Then Sam opened the back door and led the way onto an expansive back deck.

Rhone swept his gaze over the area, barely resisting his urge to whistle under his breath. Kontra hadn't been kidding. There were over a dozen small tents — most of them two-person — set up around the area. He noticed there were a couple more fire pits, too, with meat sizzling over them.

The fragrance of cooking meat filled the air, teasing Rhone's senses, and his stomach rumbled appreciatively.

Huh. Guess I'm pretty hungry, after all.

Kontra patted him on the back. "There's plenty to handle any appetite." Then the alpha tipped his head back and let out a long, piercing whistle.

Rhone was about to ask, but a second later, the answer became apparent. A number of animals appeared from between the cypress trees surrounding the area. His jaw sagged open when Rhone spotted several brown bears, a panda bear, and a rhino. A vulture landed in a tree, the bird's head turning this way and that as it surveyed the area. A sloth appeared, settling in the crook of a tree branch and trunk at the edge of the clearing.

"Holy shit," Rhone whispered, unable to hold back the words. As he watched, a large gray wolf trotted around the corner of the house. That wasn't the crazy thing, though. Instead, Rhone found his attention focused on the creature that jogged beside it. It looked sort of like a cross between a guinea pig and a mole, with short, medium-brown fur, a blunt nose, and black eyes. "What the hell is that?"

"That's a capybara," Kontra told him, smirking at him. "He responds to Phil."

"Phil?" Rhone felt like an idiot repeating the single word, but he couldn't help himself.

"Yep." A man with deep red hair, a wide smile, and a lean and toned body stood next to him. Rhone could tell because he wore only a pair of cut-offs riding low on his hips. "Took a few tries, too." He actually appeared offended when he stated, "Just ignored us when we used other names."

"You tried calling him Capy and Pyb, Payson," a pale man with black hair stated, stopping next to the other man. "Of course he ignored you."

Payson scoffed even as he wrapped his arm around the guy and tucked him against his side. "Capy and Pyb are awesome names." Dipping his head and nuzzling the other man's neck, he stated huskily, "When we have a kid, Land, we'll use those names then."

Land shivered visibly, and his voice came out breathy when he replied, "Sure. Maybe in fifty years or so."

After nipping Land, Payson cackled and straightened. He turned his head and focused on Rhone. "The boss man gave us the all clear, so you must know about us." His gray eyes danced with mischief. "You know *everything* about shifters, agent man?"

While Rhone was a little worried that Payson was asking him a trick question—where it didn't matter what he said, his answer would be wrong—he still replied, "Just about everything." When Payson smirked at him, Rhone quickly added, "I've shared a number of conversations with shifters, and they were kind enough to explain a lot."

"Then you know about mates?"

Upon hearing that question, Rhone felt butterflies dance in his gut. "Uhhh . . . yeah."

"Payson," Kontra growled in warning, frowning at the smaller man.

With a look of innocence on his face, Payson shrugged. "I'm just tryin' to help, boss man."

"It should come from Mickey," Kontra cautioned. "When

he's ready."

Payson opened his mouth as if to say something else about the subject. When Kontra issued another growl, the man snapped his mouth shut. He dipped his head in a nod before murmuring, "Yeah, boss man. Got it." Payson turned and headed toward the fire on the left, his arm around Land, taking the man with him.

"Sorry about that," Kontra murmured softly, a tick flexing in his jaw even as his gaze roved over the area. "But it's good to know you have some knowledge of paranormal mates."

"It is?"

Shit. Is one of these guys going to claim me?

Rhone knew shifters claimed to identify their mate by the person's scent. From the second they meet their person, they would want to please them and care for them. Even the human would feel a connection. More often than not, either the shifter or the human would end up uprooting their lives in order to be together.

He'd seen it happen.

"It is," Kontra confirmed. He turned and looked at Sam, who stood on his other side. "Do you see Mickey?"

Sam shook his head. "No, Alpha? Why?"

"I'm here, Alpha," a soft voice stated from behind them.

Rhone pivoted . . . and nearly swallowed his tongue. A dirty-blond-haired vision stood behind him, staring up at him with big hazel eyes. He nibbled his bottom lip, drawing Rhone's attention to the plump flesh and making his mouth water with his desire to take a taste. Rhone also noticed the tension in the man's lean body and the way he twisted his fingers together with obvious nerves.

"Good, Mickey." Kontra smiled as he indicated Rhone. "This is CIA Agent Rhone Craigson. I understand there's something you'd like to share with him?"

Mickey nodded, his attention still focused on Rhone, and Rhone felt as if his heart skipped a beat.

"You have something you want to share with me?" Rhone asked softly, hoping to soothe the clearly skittish man.

After licking his bottom lip, Mickey peered at Rhone from beneath long black lashes. "You're my mate."

The man's voice came out so soft that it took Rhone a couple of seconds to process them.

Even as a rush of arousal — unlike anything Rhone had ever experienced — surged through him, he blurted out the first thing that came to mind. "Damn, what shitty timing."

CHAPTER FOUR

Mickey felt the blood drain from his face. A tremble worked through him. He wrapped his arms around his waist as he rocked backward a step.

"O-Oh." Mickey knew finding his mate when he was so young was too good to be true. "I-I'm sorry."

"Mickey," Kontra began, taking a step toward him as he glanced between them.

At the same time, Rhone snarled, "Fuck."

When Rhone snapped out an arm, Mickey instinctively flinched. He let a whine slip from him as fear spiked through him. Mickey even half-turned and cowered, wrapping his arms around himself.

A second later, Mickey felt warm solid arms wrap around him. A muscular frame pressed against him from behind. A chin rubbed over the top of his head, then over his temple, sending soothing warmth down his spine.

It took a second for Mickey to register the sound of a quiet tenor murmuring into his ear.

"Easy, little shifter," the man crooned. "You're okay. Just breathe deep. I hear that helps your kind relax." The man paused a heartbeat, then murmured, "Everything will be fine. I won't hurt you."

Slowly, the tension eased from Mickey's body. He did as the man encouraged, the scent telling him he stood within Rhone's embrace. While human, his mate was quite a bit larger than himself, and his big body easily cradled him.

"That's better, Mickey," Rhone continued softly. He slid

one hand up Mickey's opposite arm, rubbing gently. "Good. I feel you relaxing." Rhone curved his fingers and pressed them beneath Mickey's chin, urging him to turn his head up a bit so their gazes could meet. A strained-looking smile curved Rhone's lips. "There's your pretty hazel eyes."

"You think my eyes are pretty?" Mickey whispered, unable to help himself.

Rhone's smile appeared to relax. "Yes, Mickey. I think you have pretty eyes." Then he dipped his head and bussed a kiss to his forehead. "The rest of you is pretty, too."

"B-But—" Mickey paused, trying to understand what was happening. "Y-You . . . you said . . ."

Mickey trailed off, unable to finish his thought. Sadness rushed through him once more. With a sigh, he slid his focus to the right, away from Rhone's intense blue-eyed gaze.

"I said it was shitty timing," Rhone repeated softly. "Not that I didn't want you." After bussing another kiss to his temple, Rhone pressed his lips to his ear and whispered, "How could anyone not want you? You're a beautiful, sexy man, Mickey."

Feeling his fear easing, Mickey flicked his gaze up at Rhone's face once more. "Y-You think I'm s-sexy?" Mickey had never had anyone call him that before.

"Definitely." Rhone offered him a small smile even as he continued, "And I'm sorry I scared you. That wasn't my intention."

Mickey felt his cheeks heat as embarrassment filled him, but to his surprise, even that didn't cause his half-hard prick to soften. Instead, feeling Rhone's arms around him, looking into his deep blue eyes, he felt his blood rush south. His prick thickened, arousal rushing through his body, and he shivered for a whole different reason.

"Mickey." Kontra spoke quietly, drawing his attention. "Perhaps you both would like to have a seat and talk over a meal?"

Seeing the way Rhone flicked a questioning gaze Kontra's way before refocusing on him, Mickey sighed deeply. "Okay." He did have a lot to explain, after all.

"Good man," Kontra praised, patting him ever-so-lightly on his back. Holding out a tumbler toward Rhone, he smirked. "Here's this back."

Mickey smelled the tequila as Rhone nodded once and took the glass. He only missed the feel of Rhone's arms around him for a second. Then the muscular human turned and wrapped his free arm back around his shoulders and began guiding him down the couple of porch steps.

"So," Rhone mused softly. "Which fire pit has what food?" he stared down at him while walking slowly. "What's your preference?"

"There's some of everything," Mickey told Rhone. "Burgers, sausage brats, regular hot dogs, steak, ribs." Shrugging just a smidge, because he didn't want to dislodge his mate's hold, Mickey admitted, "I'm not picky. I'll eat just about anything."

Even garbage.

Mickey kept that thought to himself. "Um, what do you prefer?" Cocking his head, he offered, "Unless you're a vegetarian or something?" Mickey pointed toward a couple of picnic tables set up off to the side. "There are lots of other things. Mac and cheese, mashed potatoes and gravy, chips, pasta casserole, French fries."

"Wow." Rhone chuckled softly. "These guys go all out, huh?"

Nibbling his bottom lip, Mickey nodded.

Rhone's eyes narrowed just a little, his attention focusing on Mickey's mouth. A muscle ticked in his jaw as he turned his attention to the fire. His nostrils flared as his eyes narrowed, betraying the deep breath he was taking.

"I'm not a vegetarian, Mickey," Rhone told him, his voice

suddenly sounding gruff. "I like most everything, although I do try to limit my carb intake." With a wry smile, Rhone admitted, "Every year, it seems to be harder to keep my six-pack."

Unable to help himself, Mickey looked at Rhone's waist. In the warm, muggy Louisiana weather, the man was only wearing a light polo shirt. The fabric molded to his torso enticingly, showing off the aforementioned six-pack.

Mickey's mouth watered, and he reached over to pet it. The abdominals fluttered under his touch. When Rhone's quiet growl reached his ears, Mickey snapped his attention back to his human's face.

Is this human really mine?

Rhone smiled grimly. "Let's get that food," he rumbled. "We'll sit, eat, and share a little about ourselves. How's that sound?"

"Okay."

After all, Mickey didn't know what else to say. His dick was hard behind the fly of his cargo shorts. He just didn't know what — or if — there was anything he could do about it.

Or would Rhone be open to anything?

Having no more experience than a few kisses, Mickey didn't know how to share any of his needs or desires.

"Well, I think I'm in the mood for a burger," Rhone told him. "I see bacon frying near that fire." He pointed to the middle one. "You want one?"

Mickey shook his head. "I'm gonna go get a couple of bratwursts." He smiled shyly as he asked, "Meet at the side table?"

He really didn't want to be apart from Rhone now that he'd scented him, felt his hands on him, but he didn't think cuddling against him while getting food would make him look like a mature adult.

Too bad.

"Sounds good, Mickey." Rhone eased a step away from

him, but he didn't release him completely. His blue eyes glimmered in the afternoon light as he slid his hand up to cradle Mickey's jaw. Rhone bent at the waist and pressed a too-light, too-quick, and too-chaste kiss to his lips. "See you in a sec."

Mickey watched the man pivot and begin stalking across the yard. For a few seconds, he could only stand there and watch. He sighed, wrapping his arms around himself. Mickey knew it was hot outside, but without Rhone's arm around him, he suddenly felt cold.

"Come on, Mickey." Adam rested his hands on Mickey's shoulders and used the hold to turn him toward another fire. Warmth filled Adam's voice as he told him, "The sooner we get your food, the sooner you can cuddle with your mate."

"Do you think Rhone's a cuddler? How could I tell?" Mickey asked, allowing Adam to maneuver him. "He's big, and I think he's sort of an alpha. Do they cuddle?"

"Kontra cuddles with Tim all the time," Noah pointed out, joining them. "And Ronnie does with Hector." The shifter pointed at his brother. "Being an alpha has no bearing on whether or not you cuddle."

Ronnie already had food and was seated on a chaise lounge. His legs were spread, and Hector was sitting between them, his back against the side of Ronnie's chest. The big moose shifter was turned a little so he faced the side table set up beside the chaise. The side table held both men's food and drink, and Ronnie ate one-handed while cuddling Hector to him with his other arm.

"I hope so," Mickey whispered.

"Don't borrow trouble," Adam encouraged, handing him and Noah a plate. "Load up, buddy." With a low chuckle, Adam finished, "Then we'll get seats and interrogate your mate."

Mickey opened his mouth, then closed it again, uncertain what to say to that.

Adam distracted him by holding out a bag of hot dog buns.

A moment later, Mickey took his three brats to the side table. He quickly doctored his buns with mustard and ketchup. Starting down the table, he began loading his plate with mac and cheese, plain potato chips, and a huge dollop of French onion dip. He eased a chocolate cupcake onto the side, unable to pass up the dessert.

With his plate full, Mickey peered along the tables. He spotted Rhone not far away. The man had a bacon cheeseburger on his plate, and it oozed with plenty of fixings, the mustard dripping down the side. A bag of *Doritos* was on his plate, and he was scooping some mashed potatoes onto his plate. Rhone followed that up with a large ladle of gravy.

When Rhone turned to face Mickey, he felt as if his breath caught in his throat. Goose bumps broke out on his arms upon seeing the warm smile his mate pinned on him. Rhone's eyes narrowed a smidge and appeared almost predatory as he prowled toward him in a long-legged, loose-limbed gait. The hairs on Mickey's nape stood on end, and a tremble worked through him when Rhone reached him and rested a hand on his shoulder, teasing his thumb over his pulse point.

"I have tequila waiting near an empty chair. Shall we get a drink for you?" Rhone offered. "I have a couple of sets of silverware in my side pocket, just in case you need one."

"Okay. Thanks," Mickey managed, unable to help how breathy he sounded. His blood raced through his veins, and he suddenly felt a sort of shivery hotness that he'd never experienced before. Mickey's erection twitched behind his fly, and he felt butterflies bump in his belly.

"Come on."

Rhone's voice sounded even deeper to Mickey's ears, and a fresh shiver worked through him.

With little urging, Mickey allowed Rhone to lead him toward the drinks table.

Mickey's brain felt a little fuzzy, clouded with his need, but he managed to pick out a bottle of iced tea.

CHAPTER FIVE

R hone pushed down his arousal as best he could and tried to focus on the matter at hand. Knowing the little shifter wanted him, seeing the way he looked at him with such open desire, he struggled with doing the right thing. Rhone should be walking away.

Except, I'm not so certain that's the right thing.

To a shifter, mates are considered the best damn gift of their lives.

Rhone knew that if he were to walk away from Mickey — even for a little while and for his own safety — the young man would take it as a rejection. From what he'd heard, it could seriously impact him — emotionally, physically, and mentally. Plus, considering how Mickey had reacted when Rhone had reached for him, the man had already been hurt by others.

Taking in the welcoming, open actions of Kontra and his gang, he knew it wasn't caused by them.

Which means it had to have happened in his past. What the hell happened to this lovely young man?

Young, being the operative word.

Rhone had never been the best at judging a person's age, and he'd stopped trying to learn the skill with the rising availability of surgery, injections, and anti-aging creams. Even if he'd been good at it, he knew it didn't apply to paranormals. They could live upward of five hundred years, after all.

"So, let's start with something simple," Rhone offered as he spotted a fair-haired man beckoning to them. "You want to sit and introduce me to your friends?"

Mickey eyed the grinning male for a second before peering

at Rhone from beneath his lashes. "That's Adam. He's going to interrogate you."

Inhaling deeply, Rhone let the breath out between pursed lips as he decided how he felt about that. He hadn't dated in . . . more years than he could count. Even the woman he'd taken to prom decades before hadn't had a father to give him shit.

Back then, Rhone had been in the closet, so she'd been safe with him, regardless.

"I can handle a little ribbing," Rhone decided to share. "Can't get through any sort of government training without developing a thick skin."

Mickey nodded. "Okay."

Rhone headed toward the big blond Mickey had called Adam. "Hello, Adam," he greeted with a nod. "I'm Rhone, but I know you knew that."

Adam grinned broadly. "Yep." He pointed at a pair of chairs. "Have a seat, Rhone." His friendly expression didn't quite reach his eyes, where shrewdness lurked. "Gotta ask about your intentions for my buddy there."

Good fucking question.

Rhone wasn't certain.

Still, Rhone made certain Mickey was comfortable, his plate of food on his lap and his iced tea in the chair's cupholder, before he took his own seat.

Momma raised me right, after all.

Rhone took a sip of his tequila before placing the tumbler in the seat's holder. Then he pulled two rolls of silverware out of his cargo shorts' side pocket. He handed one to Mickey. The sweet smile he received caused a warm wash of arousal to heat Rhone from the inside out.

Damn. Been a while since I've felt attraction like this. How can I act on it without endangering this sweetheart?

After tucking a corner of the paper napkin into the neck of his polo shirt, Rhone picked up his burger. He took a big bite.

The flavors burst across his tongue, drawing a soft, appreciative moan from him.

The patty was wonderfully juicy. The salty bacon had the perfect amount of crispiness. The lettuce, tomato, and cheese mixed together beautifully with the light bite of the pickles.

So damn good.

Rhone quickly chewed, swallowed, and took another big bite. After downing that, he heard a soft chuckle. He cut a look Adam's way, seeing the man's grin.

"Been a while, man?" Adam teased, stabbing his fork into his bratwurst.

Shrugging, Rhone admitted, "Since I've had a burger this good? Yep. Give my compliments to the grill master."

"I will. Rueben will appreciate that." The slender, toned male with light-brown hair leaned in and used his fork to point toward himself. "I'm Noah." Then he pointed toward a larger, dark-haired male who stared at Rhone with an intense gaze even as he lifted a bite of steak to his mouth. "My younger brother, Ronnie." Finally, Noah indicated the smaller, Hispanic-looking fellow with short black hair. "Ronnie's mate, Hector."

Rhone dipped his chin in acknowledgment to each as he chewed another bite of the delicious burger.

"So, you going to try to reject our boy, here?" Ronnie asked bluntly before shoving the bite of steak into his mouth.

Yep. Definitely shouldn't try to guess shifters' ages.

Rhone would have pegged Ronnie as the older one. Of course, then he considered the man's belligerent attitude and realized it was a tell. The man betrayed that he had less experience than a clearly socialized Noah.

"I know what a mate means to a shifter," Rhone stated as he skimmed his fork through a dollop of mashed potatoes and gravy, deciding to answer honestly. He focused on Mickey, since he was the most important person in the group. "And I'd never want to hurt you by walking away from you."

Knowing he had to be truthful, Rhone continued, "I work in the CIA, and we have someone in the tech department slipping information to a military division that is . . . dangerous to shifters." Seeing the concern in Mickey's eyes, Rhone admitted, "We just haven't been able to figure out who, yet."

By the time Rhone stopped speaking, Mickey's beautiful hazel eyes were big in his face. "Dangerous to shifters?" His expression clouded with fear. "A-Are they w-working with the types of scientists that Kontra's people saved me from?"

Rhone barely managed to keep from spitting out the delicious mouthful of mashed potatoes and gravy. After coughing under his breath, he swallowed hard. He grabbed his tequila and took a sip, clearing his throat.

"Y-You were held by scientists?" Rhone questioned huskily. "When?" Concern swelled within him, and he rested a hand on Mickey's slender wrist. "Are you okay?"

Mickey's smile appeared a little tremulous, but it was there. "Yeah," he admitted. After a glance at where Rhone continued to touch him, Mickey smiled shyly at him. "I'm okay. Kontra and the guys saved me."

Blowing out a breath, Rhone tried to process the relief that filled him. "Good." He squeezed Mickey's wrist gently before releasing him, finding the man's limb far thinner than he thought he should. "Good." Unable to contain his curiosity, as he brought a *Dorito* to his lips, Rhone stated, "If you don't mind me asking, is that why you're, uh . . . malnourished?"

Even though Rhone knew the red blush creeping up Micky's neck was from embarrassment, he thought the flush of color on the male's pale skin looked quite fetching. He wondered how far that red traveled down his chest. Did it spread across his nipples?

Good god, did I just think that? Really? Fetching? And I need to keep my head. Thinking with my dick could get someone hurt.

"Um, no," Mickey mumbled, his focus returning to his brats. He picked off a pinch of the bun as he admitted, "I'd been living on the streets for over a decade before the scientists picked me up." Grimacing, Mickey met his gaze with his soulful hazel eyes. "I'm a shifter and didn't have any identification. I never went to high school or anything. No home, no ID, no education." Mickey winced before softly admitting, "I couldn't get a job."

"Damn, I'm sorry, sweetheart." Rhone couldn't recall ever using an endearment, but it slipped out without conscious thought. Seeing the shy smile on Mickey's lips, coupled with the way he peered at him through his lashes, Rhone decided his oops was a good thing. "I'm almost afraid to ask." Still, he did it. "What happened to your parents? Your, uh . . . shifter group?" Then it occurred to him. "I don't actually know what you share your psyche with."

"I'm a meerkat," Mickey told him softly, continuing to smile at him. Just as quickly, his expression began to dim. "And my mob ran me off when the enforcer caught me kissing a human boy in town."

"Damn it," Rhone cursed again. He couldn't remember the last time he'd been so riled. "And your parents were okay with that?"

Mickey's cheeks flushed again, and a haunted expression darkened his hazel eyes to a brown color. "My dad was the beta. He led the group that ran me off." His voice broke a little as he told him, "My mom thanked the alpha for giving my father the honor to lead the group . . . right in front of me." Ducking his head, Mickey wrapped his arms around his waist and hunched forward, dislodging his plate of food, as he whined, "The look in their eyes."

Unable to see such pain twisting Mickey's features, Rhone quickly placed his plate on the ground. He stood, bent, and slid his arms under Mickey's legs and around his back. When he lifted Mickey, the little shifter was even lighter than he'd imagined.

Rhone ignored Mickey's eep of surprise. He rocked back a step and settled back in his chair. As the thing creaked, he mentally crossed his fingers that it could handle both their weights.

"Relax, sweetheart," Rhone crooned, rubbing up and down Mickey's slender torso, finding the knobs of his spine prominent. "I'm so sorry they did that to you." Anger on the shifter's behalf rose within him. With a growl, Rhone declared, "No one should ever run off their child that way."

To Rhone's pleasure—and surprise—Mickey curled up on his lap and tucked his nose against his neck. He snuffled a bit before taking in a long, deep breath. When Mickey exhaled, his warm breath caused the hairs on Rhone's neck to stand on end. His gut clenched as tingles erupted on his neck.

"You smell so good," Mickey mumbled, nuzzling his neck. "My mate."

When Mickey licked and hummed, Rhone gritted his teeth against the urge to tip his head to the side. He rubbed up and down the young shifter's back, trying to soothe him for a new reason. While Rhone didn't have shifter senses, even he could scent the light musk of Mickey's arousal . . . and it caused his own to surge.

"Rhone," Mickey whined, shivering on his lap. "So good."

"Mickey," Rhone growled when he felt the unmistakable feel of Mickey's sharp canine against his flesh. *Shit!* Threading his fingers in Mickey's hair, he tugged lightly, urging the man to lift his head and meet his gaze. The lust-drunk, heavy-lidded look on Mickey's face almost caused Rhone to lose his resolve entirely. Still, he managed to whisper, "Not here."

Rhone watched Mickey blink once, twice. Then his eyelids fluttered a few times as the lust disappeared from his eyes. He ducked his head and hid his face against Rhone's chest for a whole new reason.

"Sorry," Mickey mumbled. "You smell so good."

"I'm glad my smell could help you relax," Rhone told him honestly. Regretfully, he added, "But I can't let you bite me, yet."

Not sure I can for a while.

Rhone didn't voice that thought, but he guessed that Mickey sensed it — or maybe scented it. "You don't want me?" he whispered, his face paling. He began to try to pull away, muttering, "Knew Fate made a mistake giving a virgin like me a sexy mate like you."

He's a virgin! Oh, fuck yeah!

Even as Rhone's brain nearly short-circuited upon learning that information, he instinctively tightened his hold on the wriggling male on his lap. The man's movements, his tight ass rubbing against Rhone's hard cock, yanked a groan from his throat. His dick flexed, and he barely resisted the urge to rut up into the other man.

"Stop," Rhone demanded gruffly, fighting for control. "Mickey, stop."

To Rhone's relief — and a little disappointment — Mickey obeyed.

"Let me down."

Rhone tensed, not liking that request in the least. Peering down at Mickey, he tried to meet the other man's gaze.

Mickey avoided him, tucking his chin to his chest.

"Why?" Rhone demanded.

With a sadness in Mickey's voice that felt like a stab to Rhone's heart, the little shifter whispered, "You don't want me."

"Nothing could be further from the truth, Mickey," Rhone countered. When Mickey peered at him through his lashes, his disbelief clear, Rhone went for blunt. "I want nothing more than to find a quiet, secluded spot, to lay you down, and to strip you naked." Allowing his hunger to fill his gaze, Rhone growled, "You're not the only one feeling the pull. I don't care that you're a virgin. In fact, it excites me to know that I'm the only one to have the honor of exploring every inch of your body."

Upon seeing the hope beginning to fill Mickey's eyes, intensifying the lovely flecks of green, Rhone knew he had to explain a bit more. He had to get the sweet young man to see the truth.

"We can't do that, yet, though, Mickey. I'll never put your life at risk, and if I bonded with you, then your life would very much be at risk."

CHAPTER SIX

Mickey tried so very hard not to allow his upset to bleed into his voice when he asked, "Why would my life be at risk?" After all, he liked the fact that Rhone was thinking of his safety.

Even though it should be the other way around. I'm the shifter.

Of course, considering the man was older, educated, and world-wise, Mickey decided it might be a while before he could take care of him.

No. That just means I have to figure out how to take care of him in other ways.

Mickey had seen plenty of fantastic and diverse relationship examples over the last few months. He would ask his friends to help him.

After I listen to his explanation.

Peering up at Rhone, Mickey saw him staring right back at him with his intense blue eyes that Mickey could so easily drown in . . . in a good way.

"You back with me, Mickey?" Rhone teased, his voice kind.

"Yeah," Mickey whispered, forcing a tremulous smile. "Sorry."

"It's fine." Rhone lifted a shoulder in a half-shrug as his smile turned wry. "This arousal and these urges to bond are hitting me hard, too. I can only imagine how you're feeling." As Rhone threaded his fingers through Mickey's hair, he murmured, "It's so damn distracting, making it hard to focus. But we must, for a little while longer."

"Then we can bond?" Mickey asked hopefully.

Mickey so wanted to finally experience sex for the first time. The fact that it was his mate made the idea so much more appealing. Finally, not only would he learn what it was like to feel that kind of pleasure, but he would get his mate in the end, too.

"If we can work out a way for you to stay safe," Rhone told him, slipping in that caveat.

Scowling, Mickey muttered, "Okay."

"No pouting, sweetheart." Rhone used a thumb to tease along Mickey's lips, easing his expression. He looked around him before returning his attention to Mickey and arching a brow pointedly.

Lifting his chin, Mickey spotted so many more shifters sitting around them than just Adam and the others. He nibbled his lip as he felt his cheeks heat. They were all focused on him and Rhone.

Kontra sat on the ground, his legs spread. Tim was seated between the alpha's thighs, leaning against his chest. The alpha-mate was feeding Kontra a bite of cinnamon roll — one of the other options for dessert.

Suddenly, Mickey wanted to know what had happened to his cupcake. He glanced around, searching for his dumped plate. When he spotted a plate that looked like it could have been his, he frowned in confusion.

"I caught it before it could hit the dirt, buddy," Adam told him with a grin. Waggling his brows, he leaned forward, picked it up, and held it out to him. "You gonna stay on his lap while finishing your meal?"

Mickey hesitated.

"There's nothing wrong if you do," Yuma piped up, grinning at him. The penguin shifter sat on his own human mate's lap, Hunter. Both were eating from the same plate. "Some couples like it."

Nibbling his bottom lip, Mickey peered shyly at Rhone.

"Do you mind?"

Rhone's blue eyes twinkled. "Not at all, sweetheart." As Adam handed Mickey his plate, Rhone pointed at his own. "Gonna hand that to me, Adam?"

Adam snorted. Grinning, he did it.

Holding his plate on his lap with one hand, Mickey picked up his third and final brat-dog in his other hand. He liked the way Rhone continued to hold him in place with one arm. While Mickey took a big bite of his final dog, he watched Rhone carefully balance the plate Adam handed to him on the arm of the chair. Then he picked up the half-a-burger he still had and brought it to his mouth.

For several minutes, Mickey felt content as he cuddled with Rhone — *my mate's holding me, and it's amazing* — and ate the rest of his food. He listened to the other shifters chatter around him. After the behavior of his mob's inner circle, Mickey felt relieved that he could relax and enjoy the presence of other more dominant shifters. He sort of thought his time with Kontra had prepared him for his large mate's vibrant and clearly dominant personality.

While Mickey was the shifter, he knew Rhone was far more dominant than him. Still, he hoped he could figure out ways to take care of his mate. His meerkat chittered in his mind, offering all sorts of ideas.

Mickey chuckled softly when his other half urged him to show Rhone the best places to find small reptiles, animals, or succulent insects. Meerkats were omnivores but loved insects the best, along with scorpions and other choice arachnids.

Yum!

Before Mickey had been caught by the scientists, he'd spent months at a time in his animal form. His animal had easily found plenty of food for their small body. It had been during the rare occasion when Mickey had given in to his need for two-legged interaction that he'd been captured by the scientists.

Mickey hadn't known exactly how long he'd been held — over three weeks had felt like an eternity — until Kontra and his people had rescued him. After hearing how long some other shifters had been held, he figured he'd gotten off lucky. After all, the bears hadn't been held by scientists, but by witches. They'd even hexed the shifters with demon blood, forcing them to do their bidding as if they were zombies or something.

Too creepy.

"Was that good?" Rhone gently massaged his side, drawing his attention. With furrowed brows, he stated, "You seemed pretty focused on it."

"Just thinking about how to take care of you," Mickey murmured, answering almost absently as he scooped up another forkful of mac and cheese. "My meerkat loves insects, but I figure you wouldn't be into that. Maybe lizard or—"

"Actually, depending on the insect," Rhone cut in with a wink. "I might surprise you."

Mickey snapped his focus to Rhone's face, gaping in surprise. "What?" Seeing his mate smirk as his body vibrated slightly with his chuckles, Mickey frowned. "Are you teasing me?"

Rhone shook his head. "No, actually." With a shrug as he sobered, he admitted, "I've had a few assignments overseas in countries where eating insects and worms are normal." Grimacing, Rhone hummed. "I admit I'm not into the worms, but certain insects, depending on how they're prepared, are really quite good."

"Really?" Mickey had a hard time believing it. He couldn't remember ever hearing a human admit liking bugs before.

"Really," Rhone confirmed. His expression turning vacant a second, he mused, "I had an assignment in Thailand, which I can't tell you about. We were served fried grasshoppers." Scoffing, Rhone refocused on Mickey. "I swear they tasted damn near like potato chips. If it weren't for the shape, my taste buds wouldn't have known the difference."

"Wow." Mickey bounced with excitement. "I know a great recipe for fried grasshoppers. My gramma taught me when I was twelve." Sobering with his memories, he murmured, "She broke her leg saving the lives of two pups. It got infected, but the inner circle refused to take her to the healer in the woods." Lowering his voice, Mickey murmured, "They called her a witch, but I heard she helped the alpha's daughter when she broke her arm."

"The alpha took his daughter but wouldn't allow your gramma to go?" There was a growl in Rhone's voice, and he shook his head. "What a hypocrite."

"Who was your alpha?" Kontra demanded the information in a low, soothing rumble. "And where was your mob located?"

Mickey nibbled his bottom lip a little, indecision filling him. Then he remembered that he had six siblings that had all been younger than him. He'd often wondered what had become of them over the last decade.

"If I tell you, will you try to spare my brothers and sisters?" Mickey asked. He knew a couple of Kontra's people could get a little eye-for-an-eye when it came to justice. Considering they'd busted him out of a facility that did illegal experimentation, he didn't really have a problem with it. Except, these were his little brothers and sisters. "They're all younger . . . two to four years younger than me. Mom had a litter of two every year." Frowning, Mickey sighed. "Dad sure was mad when Mom ended up unable to carry anymore after that." Lowering his gaze to the ground, Mickey mused, "Maybe that's why he was so disappointed in me. He had such high hopes."

"Being disappointed does not give him the right to kick you out of your family," Rhone declared, shaking his head even as he squeezed him close. "God damn assholes." Still growling, he pressed a hard kiss to Mickey's temple. "Wish I could get ten minutes with those assholes, I'd —"

"No!" As much as Mickey loved the idea of his dominate mate standing up to his alpha or father, he knew Rhone was still human. "Don't think about confronting him. He's a shifter." Wincing, he met Rhone's gaze and whispered, "You're not, and he fights dirty."

Mickey had seen his ex-alpha do it plenty of times.

And he's my ex-alpha. No reason for Rhone to ever meet him, anyway.

Rhone glided his fingers along Mickey's jawline, causing tingles to spread across his torso. Meeting his mate's gaze, seeing the warmth in his blue eyes, he smiled at him. His mate returned his smile and shrugged.

"I won't ever do anything foolish." With a wink, Rhone told him, "I always have back-up when walking into a hostile situation."

"Oh, you have someone waiting to hear from you?" Payson plopped down on the ground nearby, pulling Land onto his lap. The hyena shifter snickered. "Waiting in the wings somewhere?"

Cocking his head, Rhone arched a brow as he eyed Payson. "Am I in hostile territory here, Payson?"

"No, you're not," Kontra declared, shaking his head even as Payson cackled, sort of like the hyena he shared his spirit with. Scoffing softly, Kontra snapped his fingers, drawing attention back to himself. "You said you have a mole. Someone in the IT department. Someone who makes it too dangerous for you to bond with Mickey." While rubbing his left hand along Tim's arm, Kontra asked, "We're gonna need some help to get the intel needed to figure out who your mole is."

"Help?" Rhone tensed beneath Mickey. "What do you mean *help*?"

Lamar, a peacock shifter, strode between seated men, holding a tablet in his hands. When he stood in the middle, he turned the tablet around. A man with a lean face peered out from the screen.

"Hello, Agent Craigson," the man greeted, a wide smile on his lips. His hazel eyes danced with mirth. "So good to see you again."

"Jared," Rhone hissed. "What the fuck?" He glared at Kontra. "What the hell's the meaning of this?"

Kontra shrugged, completely non-repentant as he continued to cradle Tim against his chest. "My men needed a little help."

"Help?" Mickey whispered, confusion filling him as he scented his mate's annoyance flooding the area. "Help for what?"

"Good question," Rhone grumbled tersely.

CHAPTER SEVEN

Rhone couldn't believe he was even contemplating the idea. Except, he had to admit, Jared's plan was a good one. He and his boss certainly hadn't thought of anything better . . . or something that would help them ferret out the mole so swiftly.

God, I do hate that it's from that dick assassin, though.

Hacker and assassin extraordinaire, Jared Templeton was technically dead. Seeing how shifters were such long-lived beings, they had to die every few decades and remake their identities. Otherwise, the average human would wonder why their neighbor or friend never aged. Being the mate of a wolf shifter in the Stone Ridge wolf pack, Jared had *died* years before so he and his wolf shifter mate — Carson — could remake his identity.

That didn't mean the man didn't love sticking his nose into everyone else's business.

Too bad this time he's gonna help. Shit!

The fact that Jared was in the CIA's systems was what really frosted him. Their systems were supposed to be impregnable.

Yep. We should all learn something from the Titanic. Nothing is impregnable.

Ugh!

"Yes," Rhone finally answered Jared's question. He still glared at the man on the tablet screen. "There are eight people listed as technical analysts. However, there are four more who are back-ups in case we need to pull in extra resources on a case."

Jared narrowed his hazel eyes, his cool attention going to something off-screen. "Names?" he demanded. "Or titles?"

"They're in different sectors so we don't pull too many resources from one area at any given time," Rhone explained. Then he took a deep breath and gave Jared the names. Feeling guilty as hell, he muttered, "God, please tell me you aren't going to leave any trace that you were in there." Wincing, Rhone added, "Law is gonna be so pissed."

"Who's Law?" Jared demanded without looking up from whatever he was doing and typing.

"Law. Lawrence. Deputy Director Lawrence Reiste." Rhone heaved a sigh, clutching a wide-eyed Mickey close. As odd as it seemed, he found the man's close presence soothing. "My boss. If you leave any trace" — he refocused on the screen as he rubbed over the small man's arm, enjoying the feel of his soft, smooth flesh — "my balls'll be nailed to the wall."

"And I like his balls where they are," Mickey stated, surprising everyone. "So don't mess with'em."

Even Jared returned his attention to them. He grinned widely as he winked at Mickey. "Don't worry, cutie. I won't let you lose your favorite playthings." Curving his lips into a smirk, Jared chuckled softly. "You did well, Agent Craigson. Didn't know ya had it in ya." A heartbeat later, Jared hummed. "We'll need twelve locations then. And twelve teams. That's a lot." Meeting Kontra's gaze through the screen, Jared stated, "This could take a little time to set up to work effectively. We have to get the teams of shifters in place to catch the bad guys first."

Kontra hummed low in his throat. Narrowing his eyes, he asked, "How many locations can you and Alpha Declan's pack set up quickly? I bet I can add another three or four without jeopardizing any known pack." Then Kontra snickered darkly as he added, "And there are a couple of places that the council would love a reason to send in operatives. We can use this situation to our advantage."

Jared's eyes narrowed. "Oh, I do like the way you think, Alpha." He focused off-screen. "Send these assholes somewhere a dick alpha is taking advantage of his people, and the Shifter Council can clean up their mess."

"Exactly." Kontra turned and focused on Mickey. "If you tell me where your mob is, we can have a couple of council investigators secure your brothers and sisters during the chaos."

"They won't be hurt, will they?" Mickey asked, his lean body tensing. "And what are you actually doing?"

"No, I'll take care of your mob personally," Kontra declared with a reassuring smile. "I won't let your siblings be hurt unless they attack us." Rolling his eyes, the large grizzly shifter grumbled, "Which would be stupid, but bigots are idiots sometimes."

Mickey nibbled his bottom lip for a second before saying, "Fair enough."

"And what we're doing, cutie . . . I want to see your meerkat, by the way," Jared stated, the sound of his typing coming through the screen. "Is ferreting out a mole." He glanced up and winked before refocusing on his work. "We're going to tell each of these twelve people that Agent Craigson has gone to a different location to visit Alpha Kontra and his gang of shifters. Then we wait for a team of military to arrive at one of them. Wherever they go, will tell us who the mole is."

"Too bad most of the guys sent will just be grunts," Adam commented from where he sat on the grass with his arms wrapped around Noah. "But maybe one or two might have some decent information."

"We may be able to track up their chain of command to find out who all is in control," Draven offered. The vampire-warlock hybrid sat with his back against a tree. An empty plate rested by his right hip while his wolf shifter mate, Vail, sat to his left. His hand rested on Vail's thigh. "We need to take out the higher-ups."

"Very true," Jared agreed. "Alpha Kontra, do you want a group sent your way?"

Kontra shook his head. "Afraid not. I still have a number of people who can't shift, yet." He grimaced. "If the assholes came to our location, I'd have to move them in a box truck or semi-trailer. Moving a rhino is damn hard to explain." Kontra's gaze drifted to a large Indian rhino that was enjoying a large bale of hay.

Jared nodded. "Got it. I'll start working on locations." He glanced at Kontra again. "Better call your friend at the Shifter Council so I know where they want investigated."

"On it." Alpha Kontra pulled out his phone and dialed a number.

Rhone was too far away to hear the other side of the conversation, so he didn't even try. Besides, Jared called his name.

"Hey, agent." Jared leaned toward him, his eyes narrowed. "Once we have our locations confirmed, you'll need to talk to your boss when he's in the vicinity of each of these guys. I'll make your phone ping off a different location for each. Can you arrange that with your boss?"

"Yeah." Rhone pulled out his phone and hesitated. "Is my location secure?"

Jared smirked. "Yep."

"Great." Rhone dialed his boss.

"Agent Craigson," Deputy Director Reiste answered formally. "I didn't expect a call while you were on vacation."

"Something has come up, sir," Rhone told the man. "Can you speak freely?"

"Give me a minute."

Rhone heard hold music.

A moment later, Rhone's boss returned to the line, and Rhone outlined the plan to him. After hearing Law cuss a blue streak at learning Jared was in their systems, he agreed to schedule the phone calls with Rhone.

Once he'd finished, Rhone realized that Kontra was dividing a number of his people into teams. He was tempted to get in on the action, but the desire to stay with the man curled up on his lap was far stronger. Besides, he would need to make a lot of phone calls.

"Okay, everyone," Jared stated from the screen. "I have a list of possible locations." He grinned at Rhone while waggling his brows. "I'll work it out with Alpha Kontra. I think you'll have a few minutes to go have some fun with your little cutie there, agent. I'm sure the alpha can track you down once we have everything in place."

Rhone knew a dismissal when he heard one. While it irked him a little, he couldn't say he was sorry. He really did want a little alone time with Mickey.

Except, Rhone had no idea where he could go to get it.

"If it only takes a few minutes"—Payson grinned broadly as he spoke—"then you're doing somethin' wrong, man."

Jared laughed. "So very true."

Kontra returned to them, a scoff escaping him. "Mickey, do you want to take Rhone to the green room?"

Mickey's eyes widened, and a hint of pink darkened his cheeks. "Um, I wouldn't want to put anyone out."

"You're not, Mickey," Kontra assured him. "When Rueben was in town a couple of days ago, he bought several more tents. Zhaul and Congo moved into one yesterday." His smile held reassurance. "Hell, most of the bedrooms in the Victorian are empty now. We keep them that way for when a shifter finds his mate, so they have privacy."

Rhone felt his blood heat at the idea of privacy. While he still worried about Mickey's safety and wondered how the hell he was going to incorporate the slender shifter into his life, he couldn't resist what Fate had handed him. He didn't even want to try. Rhone wanted the man sitting on his lap.

And I've seen the kinds of bonds between shifters and their mates. I want that, damn it.

"O-Okay," Mickey whispered. He turned a shy smile on Rhone. "D-Do you, um, want to come with me?"

As if Rhone could or would say no.

"I'd be happy to go with you, Mickey," Rhone told him, excitement causing his heart to race. "We can go somewhere quiet. Somewhere we can talk." As hard as his dick remained, he didn't want to assume they would jump right to sex. After all, Mickey had told him he was a virgin. When Rhone saw the uncertainty in the smaller man's face, he added, "I'd still like to hold you while we plan our future."

Mickey's smile transformed his face from cute to stunning.

Rhone's breath caught in his throat. His stomach clenched. His fingers twitched as he allowed Mickey to slide from his lap.

Taking the smaller man's hand and rising to his own feet, Rhone had no idea how he was going to keep his hands to himself long enough to get any talking done.

As Rhone followed Mickey across the lawn, he focused on keeping his breathing even. He felt the hairs on his nape stand on end, and he knew a number of the others were watching them . . . probably with grins and knowing looks. Rhone didn't care, though. He was going to be alone with Mickey, and the shifters were going to help with the mole problem.

Huh. So this is what it's like to have a great support system. No wonder shifters do things fast. Going slow is overrated.

CHAPTER EIGHT

Mickey led Rhone into the bedroom Alpha Kontra had indicated. Nerves mixed with excitement, and he hoped his sweaty palm didn't turn the large man off. When Rhone paused, pulling his hand free, Mickey worried that it had, after all. Mickey paused in the middle of the room and turned to face his mate. Twisting his fingers together, he shifted his weight from foot to foot.

Seeing the way Rhone's blond brows were furrowed, Mickey forced himself to speak. "Um, i-is something wrong?" He winced upon hearing the slight squeak in his voice.

So mature, Mickey. Way to go.

Rhone snapped his attention to his face, meeting his gaze. "No, nothing's wrong."

"Did you change your mind?" Mickey whispered the question, sure that had to be the case.

"I didn't change my mind," Rhone assured him, closing the door with a quiet snick. "I do want you, Mickey." He prowled toward him slowly, sweeping his gaze over Mickey. "I was just thinking this is incredibly unromantic."

"You want to be romanced?" Mickey realized he should have thought about that. "Right," he murmured, nodding absently. "Humans like to be wooed."

Rhone chuckled softly as he shook his head. "Actually, I was thinking *you* should be wooed." Stopping before him, he rested his hands on Mickey's shoulders. "You said you're a virgin."

Even though it wasn't a question, Mickey still nodded. He

lifted his hands between them, pausing before he touched Rhone. Hovering close to Rhone's broad chest, Mickey could feel the heat of the man.

"You're welcome to touch me, Mickey," Rhone assured. "In fact, I'd like it if you would."

Relief filled Mickey. He settled his palms on Rhone's chest, rubbing his hands over his pectorals, mapping his muscular frame. The hairs on his arms lifted, and he felt a tremble work through him.

"I don't need to be wooed," Mickey countered. Peering at Rhone through his lashes, he murmured, "I just need you."

Rhone growled softly, his expression turning heavy-lidded. "Your touch is amazing, Mickey," he rumbled, his voice going deep. "But you do deserve to be wooed."

"How about after?" Mickey asked, pleased beyond reason that he could affect his human so much. "I don't want to stop exploring you . . . everywhere."

With a groan, Rhone blew out a deep breath. "Yes, Mickey."

Feeling emboldened, Mickey slid his hands down to the hem of Rhone's shirt. "Can I take this off of you?"

Rhone responded by lifting his arms.

Mickey quickly gripped the fabric and lifted it. Being shorter, he appreciated that Rhone accommodated him by bending at the waist, allowing him to tug it over his mate's head. Unable to tear his gaze away from Rhone's gorgeous pale flesh, Mickey tossed the fabric aside, not caring where it landed.

"Wow," Mickey whispered, admiring his mate's hard frame. Spotting the puckered flesh on his lower right side, he slid a fingertip around it. "What happened?"

"Had my appendix removed," Rhone told him, lowering his hands back to Mickey's shoulders. "My turn."

Rhone scraped his fingernails down Micky's sides, causing

a wash of goose bumps to rise on his flesh. His nipples beaded, and he shuddered. When Rhone's hands reached the hem of his shirt, Mickey quickly lifted his arms.

With a grin, Rhone whipped his shirt off of him and tossed it aside. "I know shifters usually aren't shy about nudity," he stated, returning his hands to Mickey's hips. He teased his thumb under the waistband of his gym shorts. "Can I undress you, Mickey?"

"Yes, please," Mickey replied eagerly. His stomach fluttered, and he shivered under Rhone's warm touch.

"God, you're so sensual," Rhone rumbled huskily. "The way you shiver from my touch is such a damn turn-on, Mickey." He gripped the waist of Mickey's shorts and began pulling them forward and down. As Rhone lowered them, he eased to one knee, taking the shorts with him. "Beautiful."

Mickey felt a wave of heat roll through him, seeing the way Rhone stared at him. While he knew he was still a bit skinny from living on the streets, then being caged, he was starting to fill out a little from all Kontra's people's good meals. He'd been worried that Rhone wouldn't be attracted to him, but the heat burning in his human's vibrant blue eyes banished all his doubts.

"I-I like the w-way you're looking at me," Mickey admitted, feeling a fresh wave of lust roll through him. "It makes me feel . . ."

Mickey trailed off as Rhone encouraged him to lift a foot, uncertain how to explain how he was feeling. His erection twitched at his groin as he allowed Rhone to ease his shorts off his legs. His mate took his sneakers and socks with them.

Standing nude before Rhone for the first time, Mickey thought he would feel self-conscious. Instead, he trembled with need. Rhone's passion-filled gaze felt almost as good as his hands skimming up his legs to bracket his waist.

"You're stunning, Mickey," Rhone told him, leaning close

and nuzzling his nose against his lightly-haired groin. "Love that you don't have much hair."

Mickey opened his mouth, but he couldn't get any words past his throat. He could barely get enough air into his lungs. His body felt stretched tight, his erection throbbing and twitching at his groin. Mickey even felt his balls tighten as Rhone continued to nuzzle his cheek against his shaft, blatantly smelling him while kissing and licking at his base.

When a bead of pre-cum oozed from his tip, Mickey whined. He dug his fingers into Rhone's bare shoulders, desperate for something . . . anything. Except, Mickey couldn't speak, too busy gasping each breath.

Peering up at him, Rhone met his gaze. His face was flushed, and his blue eyes gleamed. As he stared, Rhone curved his lips into a knowing, hungry smile.

Mickey opened his mouth, only to let out a loud moan when Rhone wrapped his lips around his cock and swallowed him to the root. The heat of his mate's mouth, the wet suction, felt like nothing Mickey could ever imagine. Goose bumps spread from his groin, setting him on fire. His gut clenched, and his toes curled.

Before Mickey even knew it was happening, his balls tightened, and he came. His orgasm rolled through him, and his body shuddered and jerked. He moaned loudly, shaking and trembling, bending over Rhone's head as his mate continued to suck him, drinking his seed.

The rolling sensations went on and on, sending Mickey's senses soaring. His legs trembled, threatening to give out. He would have crumpled to the floor if Rhone hadn't kept his hands on his hips, holding him.

Finally, the skin of his prick became super sensitive, and he managed a whine.

Rhone instantly released him, allowing Mickey to catch his breath. After a couple of deep breaths, he managed to straighten. His legs still trembled, and he locked his knees to keep upright.

Mickey stared at Rhone, awe and shock filling him in equal measure. "Y-You sucked me." His brain stalled on that fact, even as he watched Rhone lick his lips.

"Mmmm. Sure did," Rhone rumbled huskily. He winked. "And you taste delicious. I'll be sure to enjoy you often."

"Wow." Mickey's mind went blank as he watched Rhone rise to his feet.

Rhone stared at him, a knowing gleam in his eyes. "You didn't think I'd do that, did you?"

As Rhone spoke, he urged Mickey to take a few steps backward. Even as Mickey shook his head, his mate lifted him and settled him on the comforter. Rhone hummed, releasing his waist to grip his thighs and push him into the middle.

"I'd never expect you to do something to me that I wouldn't offer in return, Mickey," Rhone told him, letting him go so he could unbutton the fly of his cargo shorts. "I admit, I'm pretty much a top, but that includes anal, too." As Rhone pushed down his shorts, then his underwear, freeing a long, thick erection, he told him, "Making love to your partner is a give and take. We'll explore your interests, what you like and what you don't, and we'll figure out what works best for us as a couple."

Mickey nodded, liking that idea a lot. As he eyed his mate's thick piece of meat, he clenched his chute. He'd played with his ass before, and he knew he liked his fingers in him. His body heated anew as he thought about taking Rhone's dick deep inside him.

Rhone settled on the side of the bed, then bent over, taking off his shoes and socks before kicking off his shorts and underwear. When he straightened, he growled softly. His eyes narrowed as he eyed Mickey.

"I sure like the way you're looking at me, sweetheart."

Smiling, suddenly feeling shy, Mickey ducked his head, but there wasn't anywhere to hide. "I like looking at you," he admitted. "You're gorgeous."

"I'm so very pleased you feel that way." Rhone eased onto the bed, crawling toward him like a predator. His smile appeared feral on his blond features. "Now, I believe it's time for our first kiss."

Mickey smiled widely, lifting his arms and reaching for his lover.

Gods. I have a lover.

Tension Mickey didn't even know he carried left him as he welcomed Rhone against him. He hadn't realized he'd been longing for his mate's kiss, but he'd feared the big man didn't do that. Mickey had heard that some men didn't kiss, and while he'd bussed his temple a few times, Rhone hadn't given him more than the lightest of pecks to his lips.

But he will now.

Mickey slid his arms around Rhone's shoulders as his mate settled half on top of him. Rhone kept part of his weight on his left arm while threading his fingers into Mickey's hair. He gently kneaded his scalp while drawing closer, sliding his right leg up Mickey's. The heat of Rhone's body, the feel of his hard shaft pressing against his thigh, caused an answering flair-up of his own arousal.

Peering into Rhone's deep blue eyes, Mickey tightened his hold. "My mate," he whispered, unable to keep it in. "So handsome."

Rhone smiled down at him. "Your mate," he confirmed. "Just as you're my shifter."

Mickey nodded. "Yes. All yours." Then he sobered a little and reminded his mate, "That mean's you're all mine, too. Just because I'm not a dominant shifter, don't think I won't thrash anyone who tries to touch you."

Growling, Rhone lowered his head until his lips were close to Mickey's ear. "That shouldn't turn me on so much, but it does," he whispered huskily to him. "And I'll be just as possessive, Mickey."

"Good." Relief and pleasure filled Mickey in equal measure.

Rhone used his hold on Mickey's head to turn it. Then, finally, he sealed his lips over Mickey's own. His mouth was firm and warm, moving against Mickey's, and tingles of pleasure trickled down his neck.

Mickey didn't have a whole lot of experience, but he knew what Rhone wanted when his mate teased his tongue along his lower lip. Opening, he welcomed Rhone's appendage into his mouth. He lapped at Rhone's tongue, tasting him and teasing him.

Moaning softly, Mickey reveled in Rhone's deep masculine flavor mixed with that of his own cum. His taste caused his blood to burn as he recalled him sucking and drinking him, and his taste buds sang. He knew he would never get enough of the man. He suckled on Rhone's tongue lightly, digging his fingers into his back to keep him close, never wanting the feel of Rhone ravishing his mouth to end.

By the time Rhone eased the kiss to an end, Mickey's lungs were screaming. He sucked in a deep breath before capturing his mate's lips once more. Mickey pushed his tongue into Rhone's mouth, and his mate allowed him to take control for a few more moments of making out.

Needing air again, Mickey released Rhone's lips. His own lips felt swollen, and he admired the bee-stung look on his mate's. He grinned, enjoying the relaxed while still hungry look on the other man's face.

"Mmmm." Rhone licked his lips before grinning at him. "Knew you'd taste delicious." With a soft growl, he commented, "I know you need to take me in order to bond us, but I have every intention of feeling your gorgeous ass wrapped around my cock soon." Teasing along Mickey's scalp sooth-ingly, Rhone asked, "Would you like to take me before I do that?"

Mickey's erection twitched at his groin, once again hard and aching. His meerkat chittered in his mind, urging him to take his mate, to bond him and tie him to them for eternity. Except, feeling the massive rod pressed against his thigh, Mickey clenched his chute muscles.

We'll get to it soon, he mentally promised his meerkat.

"I want to feel you in me, Rhone," Mickey added. "Please?"

Rhone growled, his eyes narrowing. "Anything you want."

Then Rhone reached for the lube that had been left by someone on the nightstand.

His excitement mounting, Mickey spread his legs in invita-tion.

CHAPTER NINE

Seeing Mickey's lean, sexy body spread before him, Rhone nearly swallowed his tongue. His new — and forever — lover peered up at him with sweet eagerness in his eyes. Rhone's gut clenched with a mixture of anticipation and trepidation.

Rhone had never taken a virgin, that he was aware of, anyway, and he wanted it to be perfect for his shifter.

God, I'm about to bond with a shifter. Never considered that when I decided to come here.

"Rhone?" Mickey stared up at him with his big beautiful eyes, need filling their hazel depths. He touched Rhone's wrist. "Did you want me to prep myself?" Peering at him through his lashes, his cheeks taking on a pinkish hue, Mickey admitted softly, "I know how."

Groaning, Rhone yanked himself out of his headspace. "No, sweetheart." He moved between Mickey's spread calves, rubbing a hand over his thigh. "I want to take care of you." Letting out a deep breath, Rhone smiled wryly at him. "Can you believe I'm nervous?"

A sweet smile curved Mickey's lips, and his blush darkened. "That actually makes me feel better," he whispered.

Unable to help himself, Rhone levered forward and sealed his lips over Mickey's once more. He lapped lightly, enjoying the shifter's addictive taste. When his dick gave an aching throb, Rhone groaned and drew away.

Rhone smiled at Mickey as he popped the cap on the lube. "Had to taste your beautiful smile," he explained, pouring some slick onto his fingers. "It just looked so sweet, and it tasted even better."

Rhone watched Mickey's blush deepen, and his young shifter ducked his head as he peered up at him through his lashes.

Damn, I love that look.

"You're gorgeous," Rhone whispered, tossing the lube onto the comforter near Mickey's hip. "Gonna open you up, my shifter. You ready?"

Mickey nodded eagerly even as he nibbled his bottom lip. "Want you."

"You'll have me," Rhone responded gruffly. Lowering his hand between Mickey's legs, he admired Mickey's erection, the evidence of his desire for him on full display. "Love how you respond." Using the backs of his fingers, Rhone skimmed along the pulsing vein running along his length, enjoying the way Mickey's erection bobbed and jerked as his lover moaned softly and trembled. "So open and honest."

"Please, Rhone," Mickey encouraged. "Please."

"You never need to beg," Rhone murmured. "I'll give you what you need."

Doing as he'd promised, Rhone gently rubbed his fingertip over his lover's inviting opening, massaging the muscle. With little pressure, he was able to pop his index finger into his lover. The heat enveloping his digit drew a groan from him as he imagined how that would feel around his dick.

My bare dick. Holy shit!

"Oh, god. Mickey," Rhone rumbled as he moved his finger deep, then drew it back out again. "Never taken anyone bare before," he muttered, a shudder of anticipation working through him. He eased a second finger in beside the first. "Can hardly wait. You'll feel so damn good."

To Rhone's surprise, Mickey growled, frowning at him.

Rhone froze, meeting the smaller man's gaze.

"Don't talk about other lovers," Mickey snarled.

"Shit, I'm sorry," Rhone quickly apologized. "Please forgive me." As he started stretching Mickey again, he winced. "My only excuse is that all my blood is in my little head."

When Mickey snorted, relief filled Rhone. Talking about past lovers really had been a fucked-up thing to do. Hoping to distract Mickey from his foolishness, Rhone dipped his head and lapped at the head of his shifter's crown, enjoying the lightly flavored pre-cum gleaming at the tip.

Rhone hummed, relishing Mickey's soft moans. At the same time, he eased a third finger into his lover's chute. Crooking his fingers, he searched out the pleasure-giving nub he knew was there.

Mickey barked a cry and arched, fingers twisting in the comforter, telling Rhone that he'd found it. Grinning, he suckled his lover's knob lightly while stretching and pegging his prostate once more. Rhone reveled in the cries of pleasure falling from Mickey's lips, filling the room with the proof of his enjoyment.

"Now," Mickey gasped, pushing at his shoulder. "Please, Rhone. I wanna come with you in me."

More than on board with that, Rhone released Mickey's prick with a pop. He ignored the man's whimper of disappointment since it had been at his request. Sliding his fingers over his prostate once more as he eased his fingers free, Rhone sat back on his knees.

"First time is easiest on your hands and knees," Rhone warned, rubbing his dry hand over his hip.

Mickey shook his head. "No. I wanna see you."

Rhone nodded. "Okay," he agreed, silently vowing to do everything he could to give Mickey as much pleasure as possible.

Reaching up, Rhone grabbed a pillow. He cupped Mickey's ass cheek with his slicked hand and lifted so he could position it under him, canting up his hips. Rhone grabbed the lube and poured more onto his fingers before slicking his prick.

Gritting his teeth, Rhone breathed deeply through his nose. As aroused as he was, even his own touch nearly sent him over the edge. Quickly, Rhone gripped the base of his prick and squeezed hard.

Once Rhone felt in control, he knee-walked forward, getting in position. He levered over Mickey's body, touching his weeping crown to his lover's hole. Rhone glided his gaze over Mickey's body, enjoying the gorgeous view of the lean man stretched under him.

I'll have this sweet sexy man for the rest of my life . . . which will be a very long time.

Rhone felt Mickey's hand cradle his jaw, drawing his attention to the young shifter's face. The sweet smile once again graced his lips, and Rhone's heart pounded wildly in his chest. His breath caught in his throat, and a shudder worked through him for a whole new reason.

This shifter is mine. All mine.

"Make me yours, Rhone."

Groaning, Rhone obeyed. "With pleasure."

Rocking his hips, Rhone thrust. He felt his cock head slip past Mickey's guardian muscle. In the next instant, his crown was enveloped in the hottest grip he'd ever experienced, and it yanked a gasp from his lungs.

"Oh, god," Rhone ground out, freezing. "Mickey."

"Yesssss," Mickey hissed, rocking his hips up encouragingly. "Want to feel you."

"You'll feel me," Rhone declared, pushing forward and sinking a little deeper inside his lover. Watching Mickey's face carefully, Rhone noticed the squinch of his eyebrows just as his lover's channel clenched around his half-embedded erection, and he paused. With his weight resting on his forearm, he slid his thumb along Mickey's brow while murmuring, "But only pleasure, sweetheart. Keep breathing for me."

Mickey's gaze returned to Rhone. Through slightly parted

lips, he did as Rhone bid and drew in a deep breath. He continued to rub Mickey's slightly sweaty skin, doing his best to soothe him.

The tight squeeze around his prick began to ease as the lines of tension disappeared from Mickey's features.

"That's the way," Rhone crooned. Dipping his head, he nuzzled his lips along Mickey's temple, tasting and kissing him. "Keep breathing, sweetheart."

With those words, Rhone gave in to his body's need and began rocking his hips once more. He eased a little bit out before pushing in again. Ever so slowly, Rhone burrowed deeper and deeper into his lover.

Finally, his breathing ragged due to maintaining a tight rein on his need, Rhone felt his balls press against Mickey's ass. He paused, fully seated in the most exquisite heat he'd ever experienced. His stomach clenched as a shudder rolled through him, and he reveled in the fantastic squeeze holding him.

"Oh, Mickey," Rhone rumbled on a growl. "You feel so good."

Mickey's hands rubbed over his back as he moaned in Rhone's ear. "You, too." Lifting his legs, he wrapped them around Rhone's waist. "Please, fuck me." As Mickey spoke, he clenched his chute muscles for a few seconds, then released.

"Fuck," Rhone snarled, a shudder ripping through him. "Gonna make you fly."

Rhone began moving. Withdrawing slowly, he basked in the sensations created by the glide of Mickey's internal muscles along the sensitive skin of his length. When he felt his crown tug at Mickey's opening, Rhone reversed direction and sank back into his lover. He managed two slow passes before his control began to unravel, and he sped up his thrusts.

With each one, Rhone adjusted his angle. He felt Mickey's

body jolt. At the same time, his small lover barked a cry, the sound one of pure pleasure.

Keeping that angle, Rhone pegged Mickey's prostate with each rut. He reveled in the sweet sounds escaping his shifter. His own pleasure soared the more noises he drew from the man, heightening his own enjoyment.

His balls ached, and his cock throbbed. He kept his hips moving, gritting his teeth. A low growl rumbled from him as he panted harshly, barely forcing his orgasm back.

"R-Rhone!" Mickey screamed, his body shuddering.

Hot fluid soaked Rhone's abdominals as Mickey's channel clamped down on him. The feel yanked Rhone over the edge with no hope of stopping his release. His balls pulled tight, and he buried himself deep as he poured his seed inside his lover.

Rhone shivered as his endorphins rushed through him. A primal thrill surged through him at knowing he was marking the man in the most intimate of ways. His head swam with the bliss of his release.

Feeling Mickey's mouth suckle where his neck met his shoulder, Rhone tipped his head a little to the side. He knew it was coming—Mickey's bite—but somehow, it still surprised him. The flash of pain caused Rhone to gasp, only to release it on a low groan as a wash of tingles cascaded through his body.

Rhone murmured Mickey's name as a second orgasm bowled through him. His body jerked, and his cock throbbed. For the second time in less than a minute, he poured his seed deep inside Mickey's body. Rhone trembled when Mickey eased his teeth free of his flesh, then licked over the wound.

"That feels weird," Rhone mumbled sluggishly.

"D-Do you not want me to do it again?"

Hearing the concern in Mickey's voice, Rhone turned his head and met his shifter's gaze. "Hell, no," he replied, smiling at the other man. "Definitely do it as often as you want."

Mickey smiled widely, his beautiful features lighting up. "Okay."

Rhone sealed their lips together, giving Mickey a slow, languid kiss. He tasted the traces of blood on his lover's tongue and found he didn't mind one bit. Rhone knew it was proof that Mickey had started their bond.

Recalling what else would need to be done to complete Mickey's claim, Rhone eased the kiss to an end. He pecked one more kiss to his lover's lips, unable to resist their allure. After nuzzling his nose against Mickey's, Rhone tried to find the right words.

"Mmmm . . . I think I recall hearing something," Rhone began slowly. "That upon meeting their mate, a shifter's libido will increase until their bond is complete?"

"Yeah, that's true," Mickey murmured, his palms rubbing up and down Rhone's back. A bit of worry entering his tone, he told him, "Although I'll always want you. That won't change after I finish claiming you."

"I wasn't worried about that." Rhone pecked another kiss to Mickey's lips before smiling at him. "I just wondered if you were ready to switch positions."

"Not yet," Mickey replied, surprising him. Somehow, his smile managed to look shy, even after what they'd just shared. "I like feeling you in me and don't want you to pull out, yet."

Rhone grinned broadly. "Sounds good to me."

Dipping his head, Rhone captured Mickey's delectable lips once more, happy to kiss the man and revel in the novelty of resting inside his lover.

CHAPTER TEN

Holding Rhone's hand, Mickey walked with him toward the restaurant. He couldn't remember ever feeling so happy, although he was a little scared, too. Mickey knew his life would be changing radically soon enough.

After all, Rhone would have to return to work eventually. Considering Mickey hadn't been in a mob in over a decade, he didn't mind leaving Kontra's gang. He also knew the group would always be there if he needed them.

To that end, Adam, Noah, Ronnie, and Hector were joining him and Rhone on that date his mate wanted to take him on.

They'd spent the last several days setting up all the traps for the CIA people. The evening before, Rhone had heard from his boss that a shifter group near Tallahassee had intercepted a group of military sent in to capture shifters. That had led them to their mole—a technical analyst named Reagan.

Rhone had been grateful for the shifters' coordinated assistance.

"I hear this place has great fried calamari," Rhone told him as he opened the door for him. "You want to try it?"

"Sure," Mickey replied, smiling at his mate. "I've never had it before."

Sliding his arm around Mickey's waist, Rhone told him, "It's one of my favorite treats. I hope you like it."

"Never met a calamari I didn't like," Adam stated from behind them. "I spotted some chili cheese fries on their appetizer menu, too."

"Yum," Hector quipped.

"Good afternoon, gentlemen," the hostess greeted from behind her stand. She glanced over them as she began picking up menus. "Six of you today?"

"Don't worry about seating them, yet, ma'am," a dark-haired man with a buzz cut stated as he strode toward them from off to the left. "They're here to meet us first."

Scenting Rhone's anger, Mickey snapped his attention to his mate. He saw the way the man's eyes were narrowed and how a tick flexed in his jaw. Rhone's arm tightened a little around him as his attention flicked to the man's hand in his jacket pocket, to the second man standing behind the first, and back again.

"Sure, man," Adam stated affably. "Let's get our meeting done. I'm hungry."

The group turned and headed back outside. With the men behind him, Mickey felt the hairs on his neck stand on end. Unease caused sweat to break out on his temples.

Every instinct he'd honed while living on the streets screamed at him to run.

Except, Mickey would never leave his mate.

"Who sent you?" Rhone demanded as soon as the door closed behind them.

"Not your concern," the guy with the buzz cut replied. "Turn right."

Mickey spotted a box van arriving. It stopped at the edge of the parking lot, and the front passenger door opened. A man exited, carrying an assault rifle slung over his shoulder. He held the weapon in a loose grip, betraying his comfort with it. The man took a quick glance around, then headed toward the back of the vehicle and rolled up the door.

"Get in," the speaker of the group demanded.

"No." Ronnie stopped and turned, glaring at the man. "Not happening."

Seeing the handgun in the speaker's hand and the cold

glimmer in his brown eyes, Mickey gasped and cuddled into Rhone's side.

"Get in," the man ordered again. "You don't want to cause a scene in front of a restaurant." He smirked cruelly, focusing on Rhone. "After all, your job *is* to keep the existence of paranormals a secret."

"We won't need to shift to take you out," Adam claimed, grinning broadly as if he didn't have a care in the world. He even glanced at the other man. "I'm guessing there's another armed dude behind the wheel, so four against six." Waggling his brows, Adam quipped, "Four against six ain't great odds for ya."

The man flanking the speaker pulled a gun from his jacket. Without a word, he shot Hector.

The armadillo shifter hissed, quickly yanking the dart from his chest. Unfortunately, the damage was done. Hector began to drop.

Ronnie roared in anger, snarling at the man, even as he caught his mate and swung him into his arms.

"I'd rather not have to drag all your asses into the truck," the speaker commented coldly. "But we will if you push us."

"You really don't know much about shifters," Adam rumbled, all levity leaving his voice. "You'll have to drag us all . . . if you can."

As Adam spoke the last few words, he lunged at the speaker. Noah reacted just as swiftly, going for the guy who'd shot Hector. Rhone pulled his own weapon from some hidden holster Mickey had forgotten he'd slipped on under his jacket. His mate didn't hesitate, shooting the man near the truck who'd opened the door.

Noah dropped, having been hit with a dart, as Adam incapacitated the speaker.

Ronnie pulled a small revolver from the ankle holster Hector wore, and he fired on the guy with the tranq gun. As the guy fell, Adam was on him, making certain he wouldn't get back up.

Another dart came from the far side of the truck, and Adam fell.

Rhone grabbed Mickey and lunged to the left, hiding them both behind a car. Ronnie crouched behind a different vehicle to their left. Laying his mate on the ground, the big moose shifter snarled as he looked their way.

"Suggestions?" Ronnie scowled.

Growling, Rhone peered around the side of the vehicle. The ping of a bullet hitting the fender rang through the air. Rhone quickly pulled his head back.

"I don't have a clear shot," Rhone admitted, frowning. "Better call Kontra. We need back-up."

"We're only charged with bringing back three shifters," the man hollered. He sounded way too happy. "I'll happily kill the rest of you and take the ones that are down." With a laugh, he added, "If I don't show up at our rendezvous in ten minutes, the rest of our team will come here."

"Sounds like his back-up will get here first," Ronnie grumbled even as he lifted his phone to his ear. "Kontra, we have a big problem."

As Ronnie explained the situation to the alpha, Mickey looked toward the restaurant. He saw plenty of people peering through the windows, but he didn't think any of them could see them where they hid behind the cars. The half a dozen downed men were on clear display, however, and at least two of the spectators had phones to their ears.

"The cops are probably gonna show up before either of us get help," Mickey commented softly.

"We'll get through this, sweetheart," Rhone stated, squeezing his upper arm. "I promise."

"I have an idea."

It scared Mickey shitless, but he would do anything to keep

his mate safe.

"What?" Rhone asked.

"Cover me."

Mickey didn't bother telling Rhone, figuring he would try to kibosh the idea. He began to shift. Ignoring Rhone's muttered cursing, Mickey quickly transitioned to his meerkat.

Sharing his psyche with a small animal, Mickey felt grateful that he didn't have to worry about removing his clothing before he shifted for fear of ruining them. Instead, he could wriggle out of them. Mickey quickly crawled out of his shirt.

"Mickey?" Rhone hissed. His gaze swept over him, a mixture of amazement and worry in his eyes. "What are you doing, sweetheart?" He even glanced over his shoulder as if to check that no one was about to see. "Your animal isn't native to this country."

Chittering softly, Mickey darted forward. He paused beside Rhone's crouched form just long enough to nuzzle his thigh. Mickey was so very tempted to press his nose against Rhone's groin, seeing as he had a better sense of smell as an animal . . . but he resisted . . . barely.

Instead, Mickey dashed away. He used the car's tires as cover and found a puddle. Using a trick he'd learned from others in his mob, Mickey paused for a quick roll in the dirty water. The move disguised his brownish-orange fur and very light spotting, making him look a lot like a big ferret scurrying across the ground — at a glance, anyway.

Mickey hated wet fur, but he knew it would help in the long run. Running from tire to tire, he made a wide arc around the box truck. He heard the occasional ping of gunfire, as Rhone and Ronnie gave him the cover he'd asked for. Mickey spotted the human with the gun kneeling behind his own tire, leaning forward and using the fender for cover. The man held some kind of communications device to his mouth, and he appeared to be whispering into it.

Probably calling his back-up. Assholes.

Having no desire to experience being trapped in a cage again, Mickey glanced around the area. He decided the bad guy was focused enough in the other direction, and he darted forward. Weaving a little, Mickey kept to the shadows and wet dirt, doing his best to hide himself.

It worked.

Mickey came up behind the human without him being any the wiser. With a quick sweep of his gaze over the guy, he decided on his point of egress—the right side of the bottom cuff of his black, fatigue-like pants had come out of his boot. Mickey quickly crawled up the boot and inside the human's pant leg.

The man jolted, leaping to his feet with a shout.

Biting and scratching, Mickey kept moving within the man's pants. He darted one way, then another, doing his best to irritate the man. At the same time, he did his best to dodge the human's hard-swatting hands.

"Freeze," Rhone ordered, his voice deep with anger.

Hearing the command within Rhone's tone, Mickey hesitated a couple of seconds. That was long enough to get swatted by the asshole. Pain exploded through his haunches, and he squeaked in surprise.

"I said freeze, asshole."

Rhone practically roared the words. It nearly drowned out the hard crack that filled the air. A second later, the man whose leg he terrorized dropped like a stone.

Mickey eeped in surprise, just managing to avoid the man's flopping leg, keeping it from landing on him.

"He's down, Mickey," Rhone stated, pressing the fabric where he bulged it. "Come on out, sweetheart. You did it." Lowering his voice, Rhone murmured, "And when we get back to the house, I'm going to spank your ass for putting yourself in danger."

Scampering to the bottom of the human's pant's leg,

Mickey paused to take a quick look around. He didn't see anyone other than Rhone. Mickey eased out from under the jerk's pants and paused by the boot. Sitting on his haunches, he sat up straight. With his front paws resting before him, Mickey stared at Rhone, offering a soft, questioning chitter. As much as he wanted to go to his mate, Mickey needed to know his state of mind.

Rhone sighed deeply as he knelt beside him. "Oh, Mickey. Yes, I'm upset, but only because you put yourself in danger." Wincing, he held Mickey's gaze while murmuring, "Although I understand why you did." Rhone groaned. "I just wish it hadn't been necessary. I hate seeing you in danger . . . of any kind." Holding his hand out, he wiggled his fingers as he urged in a gentle tone, "Come here, Mickey. Let me hold you." Rhone's voice thickened. "I need to . . . to confirm you're safe."

Mickey squealed softly, then rushed into Rhone's arms. His mate cradled him to his chest, tucking him under his jacket. He seemed completely unmindful of his wet, dirty fur. Rhone even pressed a kiss to the top of his furry head.

"Thank you, my mate," Rhone whispered roughly. He sighed deeply as he cuddled him for a moment. "As much as I want to stay right here, enjoying the moment, others could be here at any second," Rhone warned with a grimace. "Our people. The assholes' back-up. Even the cops or humans." Leaning back, he stared at him with furrowed brows. "If I get your clothes, can you shift back real quick?"

Dipping his head in a nod, Mickey agreed. He knew he would need to have cuddle time with his human later. His shifter nature meant he needed to confirm Rhone's health, too, and he needed a voice to share that fact. Plus, they had to deal with this mess before the cops arrived and things spiraled out of control.

"Thank you, my sweet shifter," Rhone crooned. He pecked

his head before he put him down, then hurried away.

Mickey peered around again before shifting.

EPILOGUE

"That's right, officer," Rhone stated, his arm slung tightly around Mickey's shoulders. "These men attempted to kidnap Hector Ramirez. Adam and Noah are his bodyguards." He indicated the pair of men who they'd moved to the middle captain's chairs of the SUV. Ronnie had laid Hector out on the rear seat, and the big moose shifter sat with his sleeping mate, letting Rhone handle everything. "We're grateful to have been here to assist in keeping our friends safe."

The officer looked over the four unconscious men, frowning. "Their weapons look military grade. Wonder where they got them."

Rhone knew that the cops would never learn the truth. Instead, Kontra intended to intercept the cops as they transported the four men to the hospital to be cared for before they booked them. The police officers' minds would be altered, and they wouldn't even remember picking them up. Instead, they would think they had responded to a call about a group of patrons getting into an argument that got out of hand.

Having a vampire in the group is handy. He'll be able to tell us how these military men learned of our location, too.

Hmmm . . . maybe I'll talk to Reiste about hiring some for our department. If we're to keep the paranormals a secret, they should be part of our end's process.

"We'd like to speak with Mister Ramirez when he wakes," the officer claimed.

"Of course, sir," Rhone replied with a nod, knowing that would never happen. "We're going to take him to his private physician to have him check Mister Ramirez as well as his bodyguards," he lied. "Once they're awake, I'll let them know you need their statements."

The officer nodded again. "Very good."

Rhone nodded back, then turned toward their waiting vehicle. "Come on, sweetheart," he murmured, guiding his shifter toward the SUV. "Let's get out of here."

"I'm sorry our date got botched up," Mickey murmured softly. He peered up at him with his big hazel eyes that Rhone loved so much. "Maybe we can try again sometime."

"Count on it, Mickey," Rhone replied, squeezing his shoulder lightly. Reaching the SUV, he opened the front passenger door and helped Mickey onto the seat. Smiling at his lover, Rhone declared, "We'll get to our date soon."

After all, Rhone realized that he didn't need to take Mickey out to take him on a date. There were plenty of other ways to show his shifter how important he was becoming to him. Rhone leaned in and fastened the seatbelt around Mickey, taking advantage of the closeness to press a soft kiss to his lips before drawing away.

Rhone closed the door, then jogged around the hood of the SUV. Once he'd climbed inside, he turned and swept his gaze over the cab. The three were still out. Ronnie sat in the back with Hector with his mate's head on his lap. The big moose shifter had one arm around the armadillo shifter's shoulder while threading the fingers of his other through his hair.

Lifting his gaze from Hector, Ronnie focused on Mickey. "Thank you for taking the chance, Mickey," he rumbled, his dark eyes intense. "We were in a tight spot."

Mickey smiled his sweet smile, the one that always caused Rhone's gut to flutter. "I'm happy I was able to help." Sobering, he glanced around the group. "They'll be okay. We'll get to Eli, and he'll make sure they're just fine."

Ronnie petted Hector's hair once more. "Yes, we will."

Putting the vehicle in gear, Rhone got them started. He reached across the console and gripped Mickey's hand, threading their fingers together. Rhone sent a smile his lover's way before refocusing on the road.

"When we get back to the Victorian," Rhone whispered softly. "I want you to claim me again." Smiling upon seeing his lover's surprised expression, he quietly added, "I know you'll need to."

"Thank you." Mickey squeezed his hand back, beaming at him. Heat entered his eyes. "For understanding."

"Anything for you, sweetheart," Rhone replied, lifting his shifter's hand to his lips and kissing his palm. "Anything."

Rhone pressed harder on the peddle, picking up speed. As he returned them to the Victorian, anticipation filled him. He'd never been much of a bottom before, but feeling Mickey take him a couple of days prior had been one of the most amazing experiences of his life. Considering how bonds strengthened over time, Rhone expected it would only get better, and he would quickly become a switch.

Glancing Mickey's way once more, seeing his smile, Rhone felt his stomach flutter again, and pleasure filled him.

Changes have come, more are coming, and I'm looking forward to each and every one.

ABOUT THE AUTHOR

Charlie started writing fantasy when she was eight, and after stumbling onto her first erotic romance at age nineteen, she realized her true calling. She now focuses on writing gay erotic romance, normally of the paranormal variety, with heroes of all kinds. With the help and support of her husband, Charlie finally fulfilled one of her life-long goals . . . move to acreage with her horses. You can often find her curled up with her laptop and a cup of tea or glass of wine, creating her next adventure. Charlie enjoys exploring the mountains of her new Oregon home on horseback, 4-wheeler, or motorcycle.

She can be reached at ch.richards2010@yahoo.com

Or visit her at www.charlie-richards.com.

www.ingramcontent.com/pod-product-compliance
Lightning Source LLC
Chambersburg PA
CBHW071129130626
46555CB00016B/1445